A Place Within the Sphere

By

TANIS MORRAN

This is a work of fiction. Names, characters, places and incidents are the product of the author's imagination or are used fictitiously for verisimilitude. Any resemblance to actual persons, living or dead, events or locales is entirely coincidental.

Canadian Cataloguing in Publication Data

Morran, Tanis, 1959-
A place within the sphere

ISBN 1-55212-426-6

I. Title.
PS8576.O7349P52 2000 C813'.6 C00-910813-0
PR9199.3.M648P52 2000

TRAFFORD

This book was published *on-demand* in cooperation with Trafford Publishing.
On-demand publishing is a unique process and service of making a book available for retail sale to the public taking advantage of on-demand manufacturing and Internet marketing. **On-demand publishing** includes promotions, retail sales, manufacturing, order fulfilment, accounting and collecting royalties on behalf of the author.

Suite 6E, 2333 Government St., Victoria, B.C. V8T 4P4, CANADA
Phone 250-383-6864 Toll-free 1-888-232-4444 (Canada & US)
Fax 250-383-6804 E-mail sales@trafford.com
Web site www.trafford.com TRAFFORD PUBLISHING IS A DIVISION OF TRAFFORD HOLDINGS LTD.
Trafford Catalogue #00-0091 www.trafford.com/robots/00-0091.html

10 9 8 7 6 5 4 3 2

DEDICATION

To J-bird—
part of a growing tree of life in this savanna

With thanks to Mike, Will, Judy, Susan, Colin, Kathleen, Tracy, Mary, Linda and Jill.

Also, a big thank you to The Victoria Society for Children with Autism and to all the wonderful people who have autism I have met over the years.

PART ONE

CHAPTER ONE

MURKY-LOOKING MRKY

The presents of the past. Which were of more worth, the questions or the puzzles? Or was it the way that poetry could find its way into almost any situation? Through the mind of a nineteen-year-old these thoughts roamed as she retrieved memories of the last eight years. *Am I remembering correctly?*

With her fingers bent, she strummed through water as if it held hundreds of strings. She let her blistered feet pluck each plank of the dock that they slid over. Briefly, she listened to Desdemona the dog bark from inside the house, neither fierce nor friendly. It seemed like that was the only sound that had changed since she lived at this lake years ago. *How did all these strange events happen? Why? And how did I, Esmeralda, end up back where I started from?* She dipped her toes in the water and closed her eyes and let herself be a child again.

The face was not perfectly clear. But neither was the water, as a frame of ancient western red cedars surrounded the reflection—a still lake portrait of an eleven-year-old. At the end of a dock stood Esmeralda Mrky, the subject of the reflection. A breeze arrived, uninvited but welcome; yet even with the shimmering of the surface water and the swaying of the trees, the face appeared undefined, unadorned and unequivocally unattractive. At least, that's how Esmeralda Mrky saw it.

"So, when do I turn into that beautiful swan?"

Esmeralda asked herself out loud. "There should be some truth in that tale or they shouldn't tell it. It's about time for a change."

Stepping off the dock, she pounded the earth with her feet, trying to make an impression on its pottery, cracked and unforgiving. "Would only be fair. But why am I thinking the world is like a fairy tale. I know about fiction—has nothing to do with reality. That's why they keep fiction and nonfiction on separate walls in the library, right? Separate ends of the bookstore, cashier in the middle as a guard to make sure no book crosses to the wrong side."

She shook her head. "Why? Why do I bother wondering about such things? I wonder about the swan, any swan, 'cause I'm tired of looking like a Christmas freak—red hair, green eyes, snowy skin which they say is so 'happily decorated with ornamental freckles.' At least they gave me a name that fits."

It held true that she could not be called a breathtaker, a moonmaker, a moveshaker, or any other phrase one might use to describe a radiant beauty. The short, thin girl had an excessively turned-up nose that perched for attention between colossal cheeks, cheeks that contradicted her delicate bone structure. People called her "cute" and "dear" and even "winsome," but Esmeralda thought it was because they were trying too hard to be kind.

She grimaced at a knobby oak tree, spotting a squirrel in its upper branches. "Squirrel? Yeah, you're the one. I bet you don't try too hard to be kind. I sure don't 'cause I've got to be real—that doesn't mean you can see me as 'defensive' or 'sarcastic' like my Uncle Stan always calls me. I suppose, being a squirrel, you can't help being realistic."

Esmeralda paused. "I look innocent, but the world has to face the fact that I'm not naive. I'll show... when people give me compliments? Know what that means?

Means I owe them one of those hard, skeptical looks I'm famous for. Those acorns still call me 'cute,' though. I can't win. Can't win? I've something more to worry about. If anyone saw me taking my complaints to a squirrel they would surely think I'm a mystery, not to mention a complete loner. I know I'm not crazy. So, what's the story?"

The squirrel chattered out a scolding. The tree quietly cackled through its drying leaves.

Cowichan was the name of the lake Esmeralda lived beside, a Vancouver Island body of water named after the Cowichan tribes of First Nations people. Honeymoon was the name of the bay that rested just a ramble from the small green crate of a house where she lived with her lookalike (only obviously older) mother Maxine, and her dark-haired, average-looking father, who everyone called Bill even though his real name was Vladislav.

Now Esmeralda peered across the lake. The time arrived to give those huge cedars a good hard stare. With her eyes naturally focusing on the lushest sections, she thought about the long hikes, "bird searches" as they were called, that she had taken with her mother the previous summer after canoeing to the other side of the lake. How they had trotted through valleys that held cavalcades of wildflowers and sweet fragrant grass! Just looking at the craggy hills and sharp mountains beyond caused tiredness to hit her legs. She thought about the climbs over the turrets, spires and towers, and down labyrinth staircases to the dusky cave dungeons of this granite fortress of the lake. She remembered how, after the challenging descent, they had passed through tree canopies, and then tunnelled through bush that seemed to protest them finding their canoe.

Esmeralda shifted her glare to a bare patch near the opposite shore. "Is that where I am now, only on the other side?" She wondered why her mother no longer wanted to go anywhere, why she spent most of her time reading or staring off with a confused expression of combined distress and worry.

She would have spoken to her father about this, but Bill Mrky, an obsessed hardwareman, spent most days and many evenings at his store, The Town Plier, which was down the road a short pedal in the town of Lake Cowichan. The times that she did visit him, small talk was the most they could speak in between customers. She would not head there today.

Time for leaving the dock. Esmeralda decided to journey down the road to another bay, Gordon Bay, home to a provincial park, in search of some form of entertainment. Anything. In some ways she resented the goings-on at the park—she could understand why her Uncle Stan called it "the vast parking lot of the disposable, the disposed, the predisposed, the possessed and the obsessed; of J-Cloths by the dozens, jet skis that throw people away and those dang Cheez Whiz sandwiches that don't have to be finished." But at the same time, the park often provided excitement when no place else could. This was where she met her "one-day" companions – she would see them for one day; perhaps they would meet again one day.

Finding it odd that no one-day kids could be found as the travel home array lay in stalemate this particular August Wednesday, and since she had spent enough time watching the sun's light and the clouds' shadows play hopscotch, checkers, and "how many rectangles can you find in this picture" over the cozy "campsites," Esmeralda decided to hike on home and see if anything amusing would magically appear. All that was left. For a moment her thoughts returned to Uncle Stan, a nineteen-year-old advice-dispenser who often made half-wise and half-wiseguy comments to her like his most recent one:

"Esmeralda, here you are approaching your teen

years and you still haven't decided what you're gonna be. You must've seen them all—the ozone depletes and the narcotic psychotics, the keen-ackies and those we call the noser-sleazes, the cowkiddings and the country bummerkins, the future AAs of Canada, the 'one pimple ruins my week' gang and the shedding clothes goats and, what they call my group, the wearanybees. Better choose your destiny before it's too late."

Considering Stan her best friend, even though she was probably not his, Esmeralda had listened carefully to his words. Now she wondered why she let anyone's nonsense bother her. "I've got to find something better to think about!" she told herself.

Almost home, she passed a house, an appealing little dome-shaped cabin with cedar shake siding and artistically carved deck railings, nestled in a lawn covered with wildflowers—daisies, buttercups, clover, plus the occasional stem of rose-purple fireweed, nothing unusual, yet a display obviously not discouraged. Two old willow trees stood as rotund sentries at the front corners of the lawn.

From her years of investigating, Esmeralda knew that a short narrow path led from the back of the cabin through a mini-woodland of dogwood and garry oak trees straight to a sandy beach of the lake. She had been told by various neighbors that she should stay away from this cabin because a very strange family visited there frequently. Sometimes, when she roamed through the adjacent field, she would hear funny sounds coming from the house—mainly short, high-pitched screams. She believed that what people said must be true. Still, she felt at home on this piece of land.

On she wandered, through that very field, trying to think of something to do; trying to imagine places, people, animals or maybe some enchanting situation in which she could picture herself. She became more and more caught up in her thoughts, endeavouring to make them become remarkable and mysterious and engaging.

Continuously she surveyed the softly blown dry grass looking for inspiration, until, suddenly, she jumped as she saw what looked like two big brown hazelnuts floating in a tall patch. Up popped a laughing face with big nut brown eyes and ragged straw-coloured hair that stuck straight up in several places, a face that had that mischievous look of a nine or ten-year-old boy. He did not say a word, just kept looking and releasing an impertinent little laugh, and with each release she could see his straight, but gapped teeth and a large piece of weed stuck between an eyetooth and a molar that he frequently tugged at. Esmeralda looked around, wondering where this boy had come from. Then she noticed a pair of big blue eyes attached to a pretty little face that was still hiding near the earth.

"Come on up, Savannah!" yelled the boy. "It's okay, she's just a funny kid."

The pretty girl slowly rose and reached her arms up toward the sky, then started jumping up and down waving her arms as though she were ready to fly. She was taller than Esmeralda and more muscular, but just as slim. She wore a swimsuit, bluejean overalls and a continuous grin of elation and seemed to be so delirious with joy that she could not possibly be real. Eye-catching long golden brown hair swayed across to brush and tickle her bare back as she moved, and her features were so delicate and flawless, and her skin seemed so perfect that she looked like an old-fashioned doll—the kind only a very privileged girl would have on her dresser.

Esmeralda could see no mechanisms for winding, strings to pull nor any other toy parts, and the girl's colouring looked so real, but she could not help but say out loud, "Oh, boy, don't tell me I got stuck within my imagination and I'm not going to come out!"

CHAPTER TWO

SOME ENCHANTING SITUATION

Jumping into tiny pockets
On a robe of memories.
Carelessly placing in beads and trinkets,
To find later when we please.

Will we forget to laugh and play?
Will we let imaginings slip away?
We will know each dream and hold it young;
Can saplings blossom before the dawn?

Someday we'll go searching the robe,
And dig for trinkets and beads.
Deep hide clues to where present treasures lie;
Where each unwinding path leads.

Will we forget to run up high?
Will we forget to gallop the sky?
Chance comes too late, opportunity so soon;
Comet catching hour, stretch it long, skim the moon.

Someday we'll go searching again,
But to sate our hearts' own needs.
That's when they themselves will turn to treasures—
Those old knick-knacks, trinkets and beads.

"This is my sister, Savannah, she's twelve," said the ragamuffin boy. "Who are you? My name is Samuel. Friends call me Sam. You should probably call me Samuel unless you are a tomboy, then you can call me by my acting name which is 'Lizard Boy from Planet

Chameleon' or 'Lizard' for short." He exhibited a proud peculiar dramatic delivery while stating his many names.

"How about I just call you 'Boy' for short," said Esmeralda in a full sarcastic stance. Already she did not care much for Samuel. He seemed just a little too cute and self-important for her to handle. "My name is Esmeralda Mrky. I know it sounds strange, but my name I can't change!"

"Why not?" asked Samuel. "You could be 'Bombastic Demon Girl Formed by Molten Lava,' or 'Girl' for short! Do you like my new word, bombastic?"

"No thanks," she chuckled and raised her eyebrows. "My real name suits me."

Upon hearing Esmeralda chuckle, Savannah released an identical sound.

There was a sudden silence which eventually was interrupted by a distant voice calling, "Samuel, Savannah, come please. I need your help!"

Samuel took his sister's hand and commanded, "Come on Savannah, we have to go home. Mom's calling." Standing stiffly, Savannah just smiled and stared at Esmeralda, her expression unchanging. "Come! Now! It might be an emergency!" Samuel kept pleading. Savannah kept staring.

Finally, Savannah spoke, "No!"

"Why does it seem that I'm the 'Savannah Patrol?' Desert three to Mesa fourteen. Do you read me?" Samuel shifted his eyes from the sky over to Esmeralda. "My sister has autism. If you want to know what that means you can ask my mom." Currently, he looked an innocent version of himself. "Could you stay with Savannah until I come back? She really likes you for some reason."

"All right," agreed Esmeralda, although she had no idea how this situation would turn out.

Samuel ran off to the dome-house by the water,

taking longer strides than his short legs were ready for and looking somewhat like a displaced seabird. Esmeralda stared at Savannah. She sensed they shared a mutual feeling of curiosity about each other.

"Is that your house?" asked Esmeralda, pointing to the dome.

"Yes!"

"Do you like your brother?"

"Yes!"

"Have you ever been to the Planet Chameleon?"

"Yes!"

"Do you ever say anything besides yes or no?"

Savannah's response to that question took Esmeralda by surprise. "Would you like a peanut butter sandwich?" spoke the doll-child as clear as could be.

"Okay," replied Esmeralda, her face contorted.

"Would you like to hear the Gingerbread Man?" Now Savannah wore the badge of the inquisitor.

"Okay, I guess so."

"Sing the song about the swimming pool," commanded Savannah.

Esmeralda felt that following such orders was part of her responsibility, and so since she did not know any songs about swimming pools she made one up:

"Oh, swimming pool. Oh, swimming pool.
How cool are your waters!"

"No!" interrupted Savannah. "Sing 'Swimming Pool'."

"Teach me how it goes, then," said Esmeralda.

Savannah proceeded to recite a lengthy song about everything one would ever want to do in a pool: blowing bubbles, turning somersaults underwater, jumping, diving, spinning, kicking and so on. It was more like listening to a poem recited in haste; the tone and inflection of the pretty girl's voice changed very little as she said the song faster and faster and as her body stiffened and she rolled up onto her toes, almost tipping forward and looking like an airborne ski jumper.

"Savannah, it's time to settle down now. Time to head home," called an approaching figure—an interesting but stern-looking woman the same height as Savannah, but heavier. Her long black hair was pulled back in a loose braid and her eyes were deep blue like Savannah's. Esmeralda looked at her carefully. Although she was not a classic beauty (she had a broad nose and slightly crooked teeth), there was something very striking about her, something that Esmeralda could not pinpoint, something oddly appealing.

The woman looked at Esmeralda, smiled cleverly and spoke assuredly, "Welcome to the world of the Andreasons. I'm Julieanne. We are a peculiar lot, aren't we? But quite lovable in a way. Thank you for watching my daughter. I was having some trouble with the solar panels, but it looks like we have things in place now. That is, it suits me fine, but we will have to see what the Man of Solar Science says when he decides to make his appearance." Her eyes rolled subtly.

"Come now, dear. We've got to finish making supper and I've got to get your surprise out of the oven," said Julieanne. She turned to Esmeralda and whispered, "It's gingerbread! Would you like me to sneak you a piece after supper?" Amusingly, she cackled like a witch, "You live in the green house don't you?"

"Yes, I live in the green house, but I think I'll pass on the surprise, thanks," answered Esmeralda, tapping her fingers together. Then she whispered, "Did she know you were making gingerbread? She said something about the gingerbread man."

Julieanne turned to Savannah. "So, you smelled what I was making again. I can never surprise you, you little sprite."

Savannah just laughed.

"What's your friend's name?" Julieanne asked Savannah.

"Elmer," was Savannah's reply.

"Good-bye Elmer," said Julieanne, and Savannah echoed her. Off they walked hand in hand.

Esmeralda broke into a half-smile. She had never liked it when people called her Elmer, but coming from Savannah it sounded just fine and from Julieanne it was passable, and she decided it was not such a bad nickname after all. She watched the pair, the strutting shark-mother and the tiptoe-galloping daughter, and wondered how they could survive together. Trying to get the blood circulating in her brain, she wiggled her head from shoulder to shoulder. Savannah turned around and demanded, "I want to play with Elmer."

"Possibly after supper, precious one," replied Julieanne. "Elmer, can you play after supper? Beware, though, that's when Savannah really comes to life. I swear that must be a moontan we see on her skin." A gentle smirk appeared on her face.

"I'm pretty sure I can," answered Esmeralda. And soon would begin what would turn into many evenings of play in the grassy field.

CHAPTER THREE

GOING BONGOS

Suppertime was almost over at the Mrky house when a single knock sounded at the front door. Esmeralda got up quickly and hustled over to answer. As she had expected, it was Savannah. Her mother stood a few feet back, leaning against the stair rail, with closed eyes, wrinkled nose, a satisfied grin and her head moving up and down and from side to side to a beat only she could hear. In her blue jeans and greenish-black tank top she looked like a young rebel who had mistakenly been given a middle-aged woman's face. All she lacked were the headphones and two jaws full of something chewable.

"Here we are," said Julianne, stepping forward and squinting. "Oh, I see you're growing a mustache, Elmer! No, I'm mistaken; someone has been into the chocolate milk."

"Goodness gracious, great balls of pudding!" yelled Savannah.

"So is it chocolate milk or pudding?" asked Julieanne.

"Uh, both, I guess. I added milk to my pudding to cool it off."

"Anyhow, are your parents home? I would like to introduce myself to them. We really should have met by now, you must agree!"

Esmeralda wondered how her parents would react to this weird, brash woman, but trusted they would immediately sense they should be wary. She went to the kitchen and found her parents who eagerly followed her to the door.

Savannah's mother introduced herself. "Hello, I am Julieanne Andreason of the sun-dome. My husband's name is Nils, although you'll be lucky if you ever see him. This gorgeous bucolic environment gives passion, which, for him, inspires work. It's supposed to have the opposite effect. A retreat. Yes, that is what this is. We come here every summer and Christmas, partly because my mother lives nearby, in Duncan that is, and partly because it's so peaceful here—"

"Bill and Maxine Mrky," interrupted Esmeralda's father in his best hardwareman tone. "Where 'bouts you live the rest of the year?"

"Arizona. Flagstaff," stated Julieanne. "We were both employed as geology professors there. I decided to leave my position several years ago, however. A real fulltime job my two children are! They are practically opposites and that drains my mental resources too much to focus on a serious career. No nanny could handle them and anyway they seemed to need one of us around. It could have been my husband, I suppose, but I decided I wanted to be the one who got to have this big learning experience. I do, when I get a chance, guide a few tours of the Grand Canyon and other fine examples of Mother Nature's formidable power every year, just for fun? adventure? to keep my feet wet?"

It seemed as though Julieanne would never run out of breath, so Esmeralda slipped in a "Can Savannah and I play out in the field?"

The idea sounded fine to all the parents. Julieanne requested, "Please stay with her to keep her from danger. And walk her back home when you're done playing."

"No issue! No question about it. We're flyin'," Esmeralda answered using the self-assured side of herself. Savannah flapped her arms, spread them far, attempting to glide in eagle fashion as she screeched loudly and jumped down the porch stairs. And so, off they "flew" to the field just as the sun was about to touch the horizon.

Woodsprites and pixies dubbed charming,
Jitterbug before a moon made by elves.
Such behaviour you may deem alarming,
Yet what are we but creating ourselves?

And the owl's amber eyes shine a low voice,
With no sign of judgment-stained attitude.
She secretly envies how wee ones rejoice,
Seems a brief, intense interlude.

An air wisp wee ones grace, holding lion seed lace,
Till a stronger wind blows it too high.
Wheelbarrow and antyback rides, a penny-sack race,
Cartwheel to raspberry feet touching blackberry sky.

They drift down slick blades of lemon-butter grass,
As the dew is already forming.
And they land in dew puddles and matted mud mass,
And twig teeter-totter till morning.

Snapdragon Hamlet moves safest night comes,
For the zabgylbeasts come out by day.
When pixies and sprites hide in giant flower homes,
Making allergens to keep beasts away.

Nightlong the wee ones dance fairy rings;
Drops hold a chalice, flow to rivers, follow elves.
Time to saunter and shamble as a slow song sings;
Tired as the setting moon's wings;
Searching free, they could be themselves.
Till the dawn,
Their carefree capricious selves.

As they pranced into the field of gilded grass and white summer quilts of yarrow bordered by wild rose, several ruffed grouse flew to distance themselves from these humans.

"Order, please. Court is now in session," said Savannah. Then she came up with another request, "Tell a story!"

Esmeralda, happy to have someone to be with, complied. "Okay, but what kind of a story?"

"Tell a funny story!"

Esmeralda glanced around, squinted and sighed, "Okay, once there was a buffalo named Bettina who—"

"And it blew across the ocean," interrupted Savannah, with a giant grin.

Pausing, then wrapping some grass around her finger, Esmeralda returned the girl's smile, then moaned out, "Yes, Bettina was actually a Sea Buffalo, the most unusual kind, and she enjoyed the bite of the breeze as it—"

"Hi Elmer!"

"Yes, and the breeze seemed to whisper, 'Hi Elmer! Hi Savannah!' as it blew across the ocean. Bettina did not know why she heard this message and decided she would travel to many lands in her balloon-sailed dinghy until she found out who Elmer and Savannah were because she figured they must—"

"I want peach yogurt."

"Yes, they must know where to find the best peach yogurt." Esmeralda looked at her friend and said, "Okay, Savannah let's go get a snack."

"No! More story!" demanded Savannah.

"Hey, Savannah, you've got the wrong kid. Let's go find that brother of yours. Maybe he's more patient than I am."

Refusing to move, Savannah continued to smile and stare.

"Okay," Esmeralda gave in, "but let me tell part of it on my own."

She proceeded to tell about the buffalo's travels through many lands in search of the yogurt secret. Savannah folded her hands and listened with surprising attentiveness. Esmeralda incorporated a few more of Savannah's ideas, but mostly used her own to develop an amusing story with sea serpents, french fries, peach yogurt orchards, crazy apes and a magic talisman.

Just as she was reaching the end, the two girls heard a sudden rustling followed by a *shhh* sound. They turned their heads toward the sound and easily found the two brown hazelnuts floating in the grass again. Beside them appeared a set of hovering bluish-grey marbles.

"Come up Samuel," Esmeralda said knowingly.

Samuel popped up along with another boy, a taller boy with round bulging blue-grey eyes, a small flat nose and practically white hair that stuck up in short spikes.

"Peach yogurt trees? How offensive! How strange!" declared this animated character, his arms moving up and down as though someone were pulling invisible strings.

Samuel continued with an authoritative air, "Yes, a break you must give us. We have traveled many miles and now you tell us about imaginary trees with sap of peach yogurt? Hah, you should be ashamed!" Both boys seemed to get a real kick out of this. So did Savannah.

Judging from the sneer in her speech, Esmeralda did not. "Who is your friend, Samuel?"

"He is thirteen years old. He just showed up from Victoria. He is my friend and cousin. His name is Spider!" announced the lizard-boy.

"Spider?" questioned Esmeralda, "No, please don't tell me what that is short for."

Spider responded, "It's not short for anything. Just Spider because I look like a spider, don't you think?" And he spread out his spindly fingers to look like spider legs and placed them beside his neck. He leaned forward and made his eyes as round as he could, which was quite circular indeed. The resemblance to some humongous bug-eyed fuzzy creamy white tarantula was almost unbearable, even for Samuel who yelled, "Yuck, stop it

Spider, you neutrino skull!"

"Let's go to my house for a snack, Savannah," Esmeralda sighed.

"Sorry we can't accept your invitation, but we've got some fireflies to catch. We're in the lantern business," snickered Spider. He thrust a finger in his ear and gave a hard scratch.

"By the way, has my sister gone ballistic for you yet?" Samuel asked. The two girls held hands and walked away.

As they neared the house rapid animated chattering could be heard. When the girls opened the door there stood Julieanne and Maxine giggling like two teenage chums, obviously getting a kick out of their newly found acquaintance. Working away in the kitchen was Bill; clearing the table, rinsing the dishes and sneaking bits from the cupboard when he thought no one was looking.

Surprisingly, Maxine, with her rough chainsmoker's growl, spoke first, "See what happens to us women after we get into our thirties? Beware!"

"And forties!" added Julieanne.

This took everyone by surprise. Very strong, youthful posture made Julieanne's extra weight look like an asset. She seemed so vibrant and had a young look to her face, with the exception of the well-defined crow's feet beaming from the outer corners of her eyes—waking, no, paralyzing rays from unpolluted blue and white twin earths.

Maxine, a woman seldom praised for her beauty, looked envious. "Something's not fair in a world where some people look better in their forties than others look in their twenties or thirties. Are you really in your forties?"

"Forty-two," answered Julieanne. "But if it makes the world seem a little more fair, I had to spend many a year being bothered by looking too young—too young to get dates, too young to be popular, too young to be taken seriously, and so on. Besides, I sure can't tell who in this world is most attractive. Human faces—lovely. We weren't given faces to repel each other...."

What a phony! Mom is sure being polite, thought Esmeralda.

As the women carried on, the girls slipped into Esmeralda's room. Esmeralda tried to show Savannah her pictures, toys and gadgets, but "Savannah the Talking Doll" became too involved in telling a story. Actually, as Esmeralda would later learn, it was a movie the girl had seen a couple of times called *The Sandpiper's Magical Discovery*, recited word for word. After about ten minutes of listening in amazement, Esmeralda spied her bongo drums and walked across the room to get them. She sat down, placed them between her knees and tapped lightly in a slow steady beat.

Savannah responded by telling her story to the beat (almost anyway, her pacing needed perfecting). A faster tempo and a louder beat came from the drum, so Savannah adjusted her storytelling accordingly. Esmeralda put the bongo strap around her neck and headed outside to the back patio and her companion followed, chattering away.

Once outside, Esmeralda led the way to a dimly lit corner of her backyard. She noticed a small object on the ground, shining. She looked carefully to see if she could spy any spies. She picked up the object and dropped it into a pocket, then really let loose and banged the bongos in a wild foreign fashion. It appeared that upon hearing the intricate rhythms Savannah released any vertical tightness held in her body, for she started bouncing up and down again. As though she had springs in her feet that absorbed the shock so gently, it seemed that a layer of air lay between her feet and the earth.

Perhaps she's not a doll, but a yo-yo, Esmeralda thought. When moving from side to side, Savannah's motion was slight and gentle. She appeared particularly unreal in this form of animation. She could no longer recite her story, but switched into singing, almost shrieking, a soprano aria all her own. Esmeralda danced along as she played, part of the time imitating Savannah's eurythmics.

Soon, however, Savannah stood still, grinning playfully and staring at the door. There stood Julieanne, poised to make her move. Esmeralda stopped pounding.

"Wow, you're really wound up now!" exclaimed Julieanne. "It's lovely back here isn't it? Maxine gave me the garden tour earlier. Well, Savannah, we've got to head home and make sure the lantern makers have returned; so enterprising, those two."

Her eyes jumped to her wristwatch. "How late it's getting. Astounding! I sincerely wonder what kind of dreams you'll have tonight after all this activity! I have to tell you, Elmer, that sometimes I wish there was a land—beautiful, bountiful—where there were no dangers, no threats, and we could send those with autism there to live however they want in their own world, and they could do as they please and be happy.

"But, since no land will ever exist, we have to protect them by encouraging them to learn. And maybe this way they'll have a better life anyway. I don't know, do you? Do any of us typical communicators?" Her voice had become so serious it started to crack. Savannah laughed. Julieanne looked perturbed. "Good-bye Elmer. I'm sure we'll see you another day!" And the two were off—tiptoe-galloping and strutting again.

Esmeralda had to sit down and think about everything that had happened. The last few hours already came to her in a fuzzy, choppy dream-like way. She felt guilty about getting Savannah so excited. She took the shiny object out of her pocket and walked over to the porch light to examine it. An earring, with what looked like a small piece of turquoise set in it. She could hear Savannah's laugh in the distance. *Maybe*, she thought, *I should have played quietly with her, but we did have a rollicking time. And, nonetheless, everyone deserves to have fun, don't they? Especially crazy fun, lively fun, unbridled and free.*

CHAPTER FOUR

CHRISTMAS CATHEDRAL

It seemed that no time had passed for the girls and their friendship when September came and the Andreasons had to head back to Arizona. Actually it had been three full weeks of unfinished games, spoken songs and unfamiliar stories. Esmeralda, in an effort to teach her friend, had examined the field carefully and had come to appreciate nature and the wizardry it held in a new and enlightening way. The clear air had given the children a fresh breezy glow of optimism.

Now, however, as the family readied themselves to move on to the place they called home, the air held a mixture of delight and sadness. Hands firmly in her front pockets and head bowed, Esmeralda only showed the sadness. She never guessed that this unique family could bring out so much of her—life, spirit, emotions.

Finally viewing Savannah's father, Esmeralda saw how Nils contrasted his wife almost perfectly. Tall and thin and as slouched as a moping computer hacker, his white sheepdog hair fringed his eyes and his beard reached out as if seeking scissors. He hardly spoke, except to say something relevant and well-thought-out, specializing in giving constant reminders about ferry sailing times and driving distances.

"Oh, I almost forgot to ask if this is your earring." Esmeralda pulled the treasure out of her pocket to show Julieanne. "I found it in our backyard."

Julieanne put her eyes close to Esmeralda's hand. "Nope. Doesn't belong to me. Maybe it belongs to your mom. Hmm. Turquoise? Must be."

"I already asked my mom. Not hers. I've been keeping it in this pocket as a test. To see if it's a good luck charm. So far luck has been on the rise, but now it's good-bye, so I don't know what to think."

As the Andreasons left they promised to come back for a week at Christmas time. Julieanne and Nils debated for close to ten minutes about who should drive first and how they should divvy up the shifts. Then they took off, Julieanne driving, down the narrow gravel road that connected them to the rest of the world.

Esmeralda realized that she had not gotten around to asking Julieanne about autism as Samuel had suggested. *How could one ask such a question to such an intimidating person anyway?* she wondered. She decided to take her mind off the departure of her friend and start thinking about school, which started in five days. Suddenly, as if she had just passed through a portal to a new way of thinking, she found herself ready and actually looking forward to school.

School started an early September Tuesday. Although she could not resist the occasional urge to complain, Esmeralda thought grade seven wonderful in the beginning because she got to do more writing than before and she now felt that she had so many stories to tell, old and new. Still, she often thought of her inspirational friend and looked forward to seeing her again and telling new tales. She closed her eyes and thought many thoughts about Savannah. She imagined Savannah as a moonbeam dancing on fluorescent wildflowers on her front lawn. She imagined this effervescent waif as a flowerbud herself, a daisy slowly opening up to the world, stretching out her arms and joyously releasing ribbons of white tatted lace from her golden heart, lace that would float out and touch the hearts of those around her. The ribbons would hold a message, a message no one else could give to others, Savannah's own secret message.

Esmeralda tried to tell the other students about the spirit and hope that she felt coming from Savannah. She wrote about it for her teacher. She could not tell, however, if they at all understood what she was trying to explain.

Now Christmas time approached and Esmeralda had just turned twelve. As they often had, she and Maxine prepared for the season by making pomander balls from oranges and lemons and cloves and cinnamon sticks, decorated with fabric ribbons. She hoped the decorations would please everyone, but she thought that, in particular, the best gift to give Savannah might be a spicy, lively smell.

Maxine had looked frail the last several weeks. Esmeralda felt concerned. Throughout September she had commented to her mother on how the woman's energy was improving and how she seemed to have put on a significant, but healthy amount of weight. Then came an ominously foggy October day when Maxine would not talk to anybody. Now that some time had passed, Esmeralda wondered if, while they worked silently together on the decor, she should inquire about her mother's health, but Maxine spoke first:

"You keep glancing at me. I suppose you must wonder why things have seemed so secretive around here for the past few months, and I am sorry I haven't said anything about what's been happening, but I didn't want to get your hopes up too high." Maxine began as she jabbed clove studs into an orange. "When it passed away, it was too hard to talk about. I was pregnant, but I lost the baby six weeks ago. I always dreamed of having two children, but I guess it just wasn't meant to be. I don't want to go through another miscarriage. That wasn't the first."

Esmeralda could not think of the proper thing to say. She gave her mother a long soulful hug.

Maxine smiled tearfully. "I am so blessed to have a gem like you. I guess that's why we named you

Esmeralda—it means gem. I really don't need more than you and your father to make me happy. Still, the loss hurts like nothing else."

The first day of winter brought cold and darkness, a little hail, a little fog and the Andreasons. Shortly after their van pulled up to the dome cabin Esmeralda and Maxine decided to drop in bearing gifts of apricot brandy bread and pomander balls. Julieanne answered the door and greeted both guests while putting her arms around their shoulders, and thanked them for the gifts, then led them to the family room. She already had boxes of Christmas decor pulled out of storage. Nils grumbled mildly as he and Samuel, in an oblivious fashion, tried to assemble their artificial tree. Savannah, appearing absorbed, was attempting to create something out of white paper.

"Cut out the paper doll chain. Cut out the paper doll chain," she repeated.

"Savannah, aren't you going to say 'hello' to Elmer?" asked her mother.

Savannah glanced quickly at her friend and said, "Hi Elmer," then returned to her task. "Cut out the paper dolls, my dear. Cut out the paper doll chain. Sha-doo-woppa-doo."

"Don't worry Esmeralda," said Julieanne. "She does remember you and she loves you."

Julieanne seemed to exist as a different lifeform now, something closer to human with her sudden immense warmth and gentleness. Esmeralda envisioned her being touched by some divine yet eerie spirit of the season. She let escape a little laugh, but nobody seemed to take note. Then the women, Julieanne draped in paper chains, sat down with the girls and they all proceeded to cut and decorate chains of dolls for the tree.

"What's that wicked smell? Aftershave?" complained Samuel.

Pushing the cumbersome chains from her face, Julieanne's smile stood unburdened as she retrieved the pomander balls and took them around for everyone to see. Everyone, even Samuel, agreed they were very nice. Savannah would not release one of them and, in fact, tried to take a bite out of it, but was stopped by the bitterness of the cloves.

The tree, someone's clever imitation of a spruce, stood like a magical deep green universe with its white dwarf lights on, signaling a readiness for the final domestication. So, with sublime care, Julieanne gave each person one of Esmeralda's gifts to place on a branch. Next Savannah got to captain the placement of the paper doll chains. Samuel suggested they make popcorn strings to wrap around the tree later, "As long as Savannah promises not to eat them."

Then Nils opened up a box marked *Fragile* and began to unwrap delicate crystal ornaments—balls, bells, teardrops, goblets and some fairly out-of-the-ordinary shapes. The family became very quiet for their special ceremonial placing of the crystal. As the tree became unevenly decorated (most of the ornaments up high and to one side) Esmeralda said nothing, so as to not interrupt what seemed a sacred moment of family unison.

Mesmerized by all of the crystal, Savannah stared at the tree in awe. Then she took turns closely staring into the ornaments, for several minutes each. She heard no one. She saw nothing else. Putting her nose to a pomander ball, she took a big sniff, and then repeated her previous pattern of staring at the whole tree, then each crystal.

Julieanne grinned at her son. "Samuel, try making her crack up. He makes faces. Smiles at her. He's the only one with this ability, and, well, what would we do without him?" She watched him contort his face. "Guess it didn't work this time, Sam. Good try."

Savannah's ritual continued at least two hours despite everyone's efforts to interest her in other things. Esmeralda and her mother had to leave to make supper.

Displaying disappointment when she woke up the next day, Esmeralda mumbled as she bumped her way through the hall to the washroom. No snow had fallen overnight as she had wished, and she was not sure if she wanted to visit Savannah if her friend was going to continue to show no interest in her. While she nibbled at her breakfast of French toast and mandarin oranges, a loud pounding shook the front door. Esmeralda hopped up, hoping it would be a package from the post office. Instead there stood Julieanne.

"Smells like oranges. Hey, I am picking up Savannah's olfactory talent!" exclaimed Julieanne who looked particularly alive today. "We just decided on a cross-country ski trip. We've got to get Savannah away from that tree. Anyone game? We're leaving at 10:30 sharp."

Maxine darted to the door upon hearing this and practically yelled, "Maybe this is just what the doctor ordered!" She was emphatic. "How about it Gem? We can even try to convince your dad to come along since it's his day off. Wait, I'd better get my binoculars; could be some wonderful snowbirds."

"Are you sure you're ready for this, Mom?" asked Esmeralda with renewed concern.

"Oh, I'll turn around when I start getting tired; I am starting to regain my strength, you must have noticed." It appeared there was no chance of changing Maxine's mind, so Esmeralda ran to her father and pulled him off the couch.

"No rest for you, Billislav, we're cross-countrying and soon!" she said. Bill reluctantly agreed. They packed up the Andreason's van and in hardly any time were off to find the Mrkys' secret trail in the mountains—Julieanne, Savannah, Samuel, Maxine, Bill and

Esmeralda. Nils had announced he would stay behind "to keep watch over everything."

Julieanne did most of the talking on the way up, "I can't understand why a geologist would miss an opportunity to experience the outdoors—exposed stone or covered in frozen crystals of H2O. He'd just rather dive into a research paper than the snow, I suppose."

"Too bad Spider couldn't make it!" said Samuel, who for some reason had not been his usual impudent self on this day.

"That's okay, we'll see him at Grandma's on Christmas Eve. That's soon enough!" Julieanne replied, giggling softly.

After making Julieanne backtrack several times with the van, Maxine finally spotted what she figured must be the trailhead to "Christmas Cathedral" as she called it. They were in a good-sized set of mountains known as the Island Range, although they could see no peaks as the trees and snow both grew thick in this region. Those who needed to waxed their skis, then helped each other mount their fibreglass steeds, and the bolder ones cantered off with a *hsshhu*, sounding and looking as though white shots of steam were leaving each smooth-flowing ski.

Maxine and Savannah stayed back a second, then Savannah, rigid as could be, tried to step forward, scooted a few feet, fell to the side as if on purpose, laughed like a raven, pulled herself up, scooted farther, then definitely fell on purpose. Maxine got a thrill out of watching. Presently, Julieanne zipped back to them and said, "Savannah I had better stay back with you, seeing you're back to your old impish self; that way Maxine can get in a good ski."

"That's all right," Maxine's kind words warmed the air, "I wasn't planning on skiing hard, and I'm getting a kick out of this. Please, go ahead. Now, please, do it. Get, get, get!"

"Well, I'll let you get away with it, then. Do enjoy the avifauna."

So Maxine and Savannah frolicked in the snow together, throwing it in the air and watching it land on their faces, brushing it off logs as though scrubbing a floor, stamping at it and enjoying the assortment of "crunches" the different types of snow made. Maxine rejoiced in re-learning these simple pleasures. She spotted various winter birds and taught Savannah how to use the binoculars to see chickadees, Steller's jays, and a bald eagle.

After about an hour of this romping, the rest of the group came back to rejoin them. Bill's normally tawny cheeks shined with sweat and wore a shade of red that approached ruby. Between sips from his water bottle he said, "Wow, the day has come, I knew it would, when I can no longer keep up with our Little Gem. Anyway, how are you two doing? Wanted to see if you're getting hungry. Julieanne packed some sandwiches, you know."

"We've been having a blast," stated Maxine, "but lunch sounds great about now. I put some dried fruit and cookies in your pack, Bill. I'm surprised they're still there, or are they? Oh, I do enjoy ribbing a well-built man."

After a quick lunch the time came to get the blood circulating again. The three youths, already cavorting about, tossed snow dust at each other, did somersaults and handstands and played leapfrog in luminous snow dunes. Julieanne insisted on staying back with Savannah, while the rest went on. They agreed everyone would meet again in an hour and a half. Neither Bill nor Maxine felt like pushing it too hard. They chatted quietly as their skis crept through the powder. That left Esmeralda and Samuel to race ahead of the others to find the thrill, the exhilaration of continuous acceleration through the white drifting veil.

After the two racers had exhausted themselves, Samuel looked at Esmeralda with a charming little expression and said, "Gem, you can tell me one of your stories. I wouldn't mind hearing an adventure; bring on those dragons or knights or space critters or upside-down people or something really bizarre."

Esmeralda replied, "How about the story about the little blonde boy who was too cute and smart for his own windpants." The adrenaline had been running through her system and she could not hold back the urge to be persnickety. "Don't mock me and my stories, little Lizard Boy."

Samuel stood silent a few seconds, then sighed, "Oh, okay, no story. Should we head back now?"

They turned around quickly. A moment later Samuel gave a fake smile to Esmeralda and said, "I'll tell you a story, then. It's called 'The Girl who was Too Shallow to Need Snow Gaiters'." Esmeralda made a sudden surge ahead. A fast pace was held, but she continued to hear exhausted breathing behind her and little phrases from a very weird story.

Fifteen minutes later they spotted Bill and Maxine.

"The end!" exclaimed Samuel.

Delight filled Maxine's face when she saw them, and she yelled, "Good timing, kiddos, I was starting to worry. Seems the snowfall is a-walloping and so is the wind. I believe it's getting darker too." Another fifteen minutes passed before they caught sight of Julieanne and Savannah, skis still on, holding hands and doing a dance.

"Twist the blizzard away!" were the lyrics heard shouted as they approached.

"Mom, you embarrass me sometimes!" moaned Samuel.

"Well, my dear lizard child, we had to do something to make your return a safe one. Feel that chill? Let's get back to the van."

Five minutes later, as the group reached the van, visibility became poor. Immediately, like well-trained roadies, they loaded up for a long drive home. Maxine sat silently in the front so as not to disturb Julieanne's cautious driving. Bill sat beside Samuel on the middle seat and told him all about the pros and cons of running a hardware store.

"You'll have to come visit The Town Plier before you go, young man," said Bill proudly. "It's a dream come to life for me. It's almost a museum. We've got this great display of tools and farm implements from the early 1900s, before modern machinery did so much of our work. The smaller of those we keep behind the glass. We've got the latest in everything too! Great gifts if you haven't finished your Christmas shopping. Oh, yes, best hardware store I've ever seen!"

Savannah and Esmeralda were curled up together in the backseat, whispering stories to each other so that Samuel could not hear them. Occasionally Savannah squealed with delight, and the other four passengers would look at her with fingers to their lips, simultaneously whispering "shhh," and her mother would say, almost singing, "regular voice." Savannah complied until excitement, again, took away her self-control.

At one point Julieanne stopped at a pullout, opened the glove box, took out a pair of earplugs and calmly put them in her ears. She turned to Maxine and said, "If there is anything I should hear, please inform me," as she slowly steered the van back onto the road.

By the time they returned home all the passengers had fallen asleep except Savannah, who quietly stared out the window at the movement of the feathery flakes.

For the Andreasons the next day brought Christmas shopping in the nearby festive village of Chemainus. Esmeralda decided to tag along even though she had made all her Christmas presents this year.

On the way she pointed at her dad's hardware store. "Oh, I knew that," said Nils. "I go there all the time." They decided to stop and do a quick survey of the merchandise. Greeting them with a big face-breaking grin, Bill spread his handshake as if passing out candy and proceeded to give Samuel the tour of his world.

The first stop was his brother and Esmeralda's uncle, Stan, who wore the title of "Assistant Manager" on his fingerprint-covered nametag. Stan pointed out the model train that circled the interior of the store, which kept the visitors gazing upward for some time. Nils was especially interested in Stan's lecture on turn-of-the-century artifacts, but the lessons Bill gave Samuel on how to use today's tools got impossibly long. Surprisingly, Savannah stood like an artifact herself. It was most trying, however, for the kin to be patient, and it would have been a challenge to tell which was the most wired, Esmeralda or the lighting display she was standing beside.

Julieanne looked innocently at Nils. Nils surveyed the store. Stan smirked at Esmeralda. Esmeralda's eyes wove a laser pattern between Savannah and the other Andreasons. Julieanne watched Esmeralda do so. Savannah continued to stand still. Esmeralda, prepared for anything, waited for her to do something different. Savannah started to chirp. An hour and a quarter after arriving, the visitors made their escape.

Chemainus held many delightful gift shops and toy stores and cozy restaurants. Nils and Julieanne became the debating amateur art critics as they viewed the assorted styles of murals that decorated the sides of the buildings. Julieanne preferred the native portraits; Nils gave the most stars to the murals with maritime themes. For some time the group forgot that they were there to shop and not just to behold, sniff and listen to the medley of sights, smells and sounds of the season.

Upon entering each store Esmeralda watched to see which behaviours Savannah would exhibit and which reactions she would elicit. Toy stores generally excited her, mainly because of the activity level, but they also held people who were often oblivious to her. The more expensive the merchandise, however, the more extensive the stare, and the tighter the bodies and lips were, and as a result, the more anxious Savannah became. If Julieanne were a dog, her ears would have been at full perk, and her nose would have been on alert. As it was, she was always in a prime shepherding position.

In one toy store Savannah became excited when Esmeralda made some stuffed animals dance to the music. Her non-stop laughter bordered on shrill, which her mother quietly tried to encourage back to a softer level of sound. Another mother grumbled to her own daughter, "I'm glad you don't behave like that girl."

Julieanne froze, except for her eyes which shifted toward the woman. A minute later she turned to Esmeralda and said, "Maybe I should have said something, but sometimes I just don't feel I have the patience to deal with women of that sort."

When it became dark, everyone admitted to being tired and stimulated-a-plenty except for Savannah, who protested the impending departure with whining, tears and a shaking tenseness. This place, with all its sensations, intoxicated the child to a point where reasoning could not change her focus. Away from the group she bolted and into a gift shop she dashed, approaching the cashier, screaming, "I want my mommy! Mean, mean, mean! I want my mommy!"

Julieanne had followed her in and upon hearing her screams explained, "I'm her mother. I'm sorry about this. She's just upset."

"No! I want my nice mommy!" yelled Savannah.

Esmeralda, who had also followed, spoke up, "That

really is her mom."

The cashier gave Julieanne a perplexed scowl. Julieanne opened her purse and pulled out her passport without hesitation, Savannah's too. She showed them to the cashier, who carefully eyed the names and pictures.

"She certainly looks like you, and you do have the same last name." The cashier laughed, "I'm so relieved I don't have to call the police. For a minute there my heart pounded like a judge's gavel during a blackout in the middle of a full solar eclipse."

"My apologies, Miss!" said Julieanne. "Glad you checked."

When she thought Julieanne wasn't looking, the cashier shook her head and shivered.

Julieanne had, in fact, seen her and said, "Why did you have to ruin a pleasant ending?"

The cashier looked straight at Julieanne. With absolute sheepishness, she said, "I hope your daughter gets better!"

"Thank you," said Julieanne, quietly.

Suddenly Savannah ran to a table and grabbed a teacup and almost put it to her mouth. Her mother's gentle, but quick grasp played interference.

Finally, Julieanne took Savannah outside and got her to stand in a quiet corner so she could talk to her. "Darling, relax. It's okay. Breathe." Savannah clenched her jacket and shook. Julieanne said, "Just think about crazy old Frosty the Snowman. You just never know with that guy."

"You never, never know," said Savannah in a soft falsetto.

"Here, have a few jelly berries. You hungry?"

"Yes. You never, never know."

Shortly after, the girl quietly walked with the group, Esmeralda's arm around her, as they avoided the busy areas and found their van.

Esmeralda did not see any more of the Andreasons that season. The next day they headed off for Savannah's grandmother's house in the town of Duncan. Then, unexpectedly, after Christmas they spent several days in Victoria visiting and admiring the "mansion" that Spider's family had recently moved into. Following that visit, Arizona drew them back.

A week later, with no warning, a *FOR SALE* sign appeared in front of the dome cabin.

CHAPTER FIVE

SARSAPARILLA SUMMER

Winter took forever, spring took even longer, and then the blossoms of summer arrived and Esmeralda wondered, how she wondered, if and when the dome cabin would loose its emptiness and she would again hear strange yet familiar sounds coming from it. The *FOR SALE* sign had stood as stubbornly as Esmeralda throughout the spring, as though it knew it would eventually win and then come down appropriately.

Every time she walked past the sign Esmeralda gave it a push, just enough to weaken it and help postpone her doubt. One day she hauled her old Kidplay-brand tent out of storage and set it behind the sign. *Maybe, they'll all think this crummy little tent is what's being sold*, she snickered to herself, then came up with another idea. She remembered seeing some white paint in the storage shed. Quietly, she retrieved a can and a brush and took them to the sign. On the words *FOR SALE* she carefully painted over the letters *O*, *R* and *S*, leaving *F* and *ALE* for all to see. *Well, "fail" really is one of those words that ought to be misspelled, right world?* Esmeralda went inside her little tent and fell asleep, for around an hour.

When she came out of the tent she took another look at the sign. "I really did paint it. What got into me? What will they think? Nobody ever drives by. Maybe this, too, shall go unnoticed." She went inside her house and got a pen and paper and took it with her inside the tent. She tried to think of how she could write a letter of apology and to whom she should write it. Finally, she wrote, "I still believe you will return. Maybe you will." She crumpled up the note, threw it and hit the sign, then packed up her tent, the paint, the brush and took them back home with her, whispering a little tune, "Maybe, maybe, maybe."

It happened. July seventh was the day. Esmeralda lifted the curtains of her window and recognized the van that rested at the cabin, then saw Savannah and Samuel playfully approaching her house. She raced out and gave Savannah a welcoming hug. Savannah stood stiffly, but smiled and said, "Elmer came back!"

"No, Savannah Banana, we came back! Esmeralda will be here forever," said Samuel.

"What is that supposed to mean, 'forever'?" Esmeralda responded. "And where did the name Savannah Banana come from?"

Samuel appeared to have difficulty deciding whether or not to be friendly. The tone of his words kept changing while he spoke, "I just mean that *you* don't have to spend half your life in a car. You don't have any plans to go anywhere, do you? And Savannah Banana? That's been her play name for a long time. It's actually Savannah Banana Santana 'cause she likes drum music, you knew that, didn't you?"

"Knew what? I knew that she liked drum music," answered Esmeralda. "How did you know about Santana though?"

"I don't know how I knew. I just knew. How did you know?" Samuel had returned to his antagonistic self.

"Who says I knew?" answered his adversary, not daring to admit to this decoy of a boy that she sometimes listened to her parents' CDs.

"You must've known. You recognized the name, didn't you?"

Esmeralda turned to her friend, "Ready to play in the field Savannah?"

Savannah smiled a definite yes, and the girls picked up where they had left off the previous summer.

Samuel went up to the Mrky house to say hello. Bill

showed tremendous pleasure at seeing the lad, and proceeded to give him the update on the hardware store.

"Hope you don't move, kid. My nutty wife gets some faraway ideas about moving sometimes, but I love my store, I can't imagine life without it."

Meanwhile Maxine, whose moods had been up and down lately, had made it to the dome and hooked up with Julieanne, who was preparing to head off to get groceries.

"I know, instead of making a shopping list right now, let's make a list of all the things we can do this summer, eh?" suggested Julieanne. "Boys and girls, girls and boys, a fantastic summer, yes, that's what this will be. Believe it my dear friend. If Nils doesn't want to do anything, that's his loss. I even had this idea that you and I could leave the kids with the men for a weekend and hit Victoria, perhaps when there's a great concert or play in town; or maybe even Vancouver. What d'ya say kiddo? I'd be willing to pay Esmeralda to help keep an eye on my kids."

"Exceptional! That's all I have to say on the subject." A change of pace sounded just fine to Maxine, who had almost completely focused on being a wife and mother for over twelve years. "And I'm sure Esmeralda would not object to lending a hand. But you don't need to pay her."

"Well, I'll have to compensate her somehow."

"Oh, I'm sure we will." Maxine let out a chuckle.

Marching outside and declaring, "Fail!" Julieanne plucked the *FOR SALE* sign from the lawn and threw it aside.

"Nils says it's too far to drive. I say 'Let's fly!' He says, 'Too expensive!' He wants the money to buy a fancier house in Arid-Zona. But look at him sleeping in the hammock. When he wakes up he'll realize how much he loves it here. We go through this every year. I just hope it never sells when he's going through one of his phases.... And secretly I thank Esmeralda for her artwork. She's much like me when I was her age, but probably not as severe. Let's hope, anyway. I could always be counted on to put an extra turkey on the table, if you know what I mean. Oh, I remember one time..."

While Julieanne continued to speak, Maxine lifted herself with an air of lightness, ran home and quickly returned with newspaper supplements on island events she had saved to use as a reference if she found herself in times of travel. The women proceeded to make a list so long that they would have had to be professional calendar jugglers to coordinate such a complex schedule. This exercise in planning gave Maxine an unexpected sense of gratification. She felt herself beam and as she put her hands to her warm cheeks, she wondered if Julieanne had observed or if anyone would notice her revival.

From in the field, Esmeralda had watched Julieanne's usurping of the *FOR SALE* sign and with it felt several months of concern lift away. She would have more than memories. Then she and Savannah exchanged more stories, and Esmeralda brought out her bongos to play for "Ms. Santana," plus some plastic containers for Savannah to pound on if she wanted to. Savannah did not. She just wanted to listen.

Savannah stared at the ground for a few minutes, then picked up a stone, as green and shiny as the lake. The girls took turns looking at it.

Eventually, Savannah spoke up. "Take a trip to China!" she said.

"Yeah, maybe it's jade," said Esmeralda.

"Take a trip to China."

"Who, me or you?"

"Elmer and Savannah Banana."

"How do we get there, oh great Savannah Banana?"

"Take a left turn at Portland." Savannah took her friend's hand and led her, Esmeralda trying to keep up with her quick feet, to a corner of the field. They made a sharp left turn.

"What's next?" asked Esmeralda.

"Take a right turn at Scotland." They ran several strides then turned to the right.

"Then?"

"Take a left turn at Majestic."

"Where's Majestic?"

"There," said Savannah, pointing two metres ahead. They moved up and turned left.

"Right turn at pizza. Right there, turn at pizza. Right there." She pointed as she continued to lead her friend. "Take a left turn at information. I want some information." She ran a few more steps. "Elmer takes a left turn at the swimming pool." And the girls hastened all the way to the lake before turning left.

They skipped beside the lake until Esmeralda started to slow down. She panted, "Are we in China yet?"

"Yes!" declared Savannah.

"Savannah, do you know what? I think you're very smart."

"Savannah is too smart!"

"I think you might have something there," said Esmeralda. "I think you are so smart I will no longer call you Savannah and especially not Savannah Banana, but I will call you 'Savvy' instead. Do you know what 'Savvy' means? I think it kind of means a smart person who knows a lot about what's going on or something like that."

"Savvy has dreams," the girl revealed.

"What do you see when you dream?"

"Purple and black and pink and black and blue and black. Find the turquoise. Hear the triangle music."

"Is it pretty?"

"Yes!" stated Savvy.

The next morning arrived with a surge of heat that warmed Esmeralda's bedroom. She wanted to sleep in, for she had stayed up fairly late with her friend, but she couldn't find a comfortable position for her body to lie in and her mind became too active. Giving up, she arose. After a quick breakfast she hurried out to the field. There Savvy and the lizard boy were attempting to fly a kite.

"Not windy enough!" Esmeralda yelled out.

"I know that," said Samuel, "but Savannah spotted the kite and wanted to fly it and Mom, that lady of land and sea and air, that's what dad calls her, said we should give it a try and see if the wind picks up. It's as still as a corpse out here. Who was she trying to fool! Guess we were a little too wild in the house this morning. Anyway, if I'm out here I'll be able to see when Spider shows up!"

The three decided to put their noses to the field and see if this summer would bring any new and quizzical species. It was almost noon by the time the Weatherbys pulled up in their unblemished station wagon: Spider, his mother Elspeth, his father Lawrence, and his baby sister Diamanta. Esmeralda mumbled to herself, trying to guess what Spider's real name was. "Chauncy? Kingsley? Billingsley? Rutherford?"

"Great day for swimming, eh Spider?" Samuel greeted his friend with a handshake. He appeared dwarfed by Spider, whose chin now rested at the height that the top of his head had just skimmed last summer.

"Why the handshake, Lizard? We aren't adults yet," said Spider in his usual squeaky nasal tone.

"I just wanted to test your hand to see if you've been working or living the life of luxury," replied Samuel. "I guess all this mansion living must be driving you crazy."

"No, it's not too bad. Just wish we had a sloppy area of lawn I could muck about in. To make changes to."

Spider sighed. "This should be a refreshing two weeks. It'll be good to get away from Diamanta, too. She's really spoiled! Hey, I brought my flute along. I'll play it for you in the woods and we can pretend we belong to a band of minstrel men of mirth and adventure; you know, search for enchanted mugs or tumblers or whatever. Rescue maidens in need. Should've brought my guitar along for you to play. Oh, well. Hey, I'm hungry. Let's see what lies ahead for us in your kitchen."

After lunch Savannah and Esmeralda took an interest in Diamanta, a cherub of sixteen months who was dressed in a frilly rose-coloured frock of linen embellished with burgundy smocking.

Savannah smiled at the baby and gently cooed, "Hi! My name is Lance Ajax. Hi! My name is Trudy Poodjky. Hi! My name is Rocky and Bullwinkle." Then she sat down and vigorously rubbed her hands through the grass.

Elspeth was keeping a close eye on the situation, particularly all aspects of Savannah's behaviour. After roughly five minutes she swooped up Diamanta and said, "We must return home now. We have an engagement this evening. It was nice to meet you Esmeralda." Then she and her husband said good-bye to Julieanne and were gone.

Julieanne stared at the retreating station wagon and commented, "If she weren't my sister I'd think she was some kind of uppity slime-ridden creature."

Esmeralda thought she knew what Julieanne meant, but decided not to worry about it and to just go get ready for this summer's inaugural lake swim. When she looked over her shoulder she was surprised to see Savvy had already changed into her becoming bright purple racing swimsuit and aqua socks. Esmeralda ran home to put on her swim tee-shirt and cut-offs.

By the time Esmeralda arrived at the lake the lizard-boy and Spider were paddling a canoe, and encircling some extraordinary lake creature they seemed to have trapped. A moment later she heard the creature make various little laughing sounds, and she realized it was Savvy, playing the game, enjoying the feel of the water and showing a sudden freedom of movement. She reminded Esmeralda of a dolphin, or perhaps a sea otter, the way she twisted and flipped underwater, no movement impossible, appearing to be frivolously swimming in a bubbly sea of sarsaparilla.

"If only we could get this specimen in the boat, I'm sure the curator of the museum would go wild over seeing her," Samuel said with his most adventurous flair. "Of course, we would insist that she be set free again, because humanitarians we truly are. Am I right, my friend?"

"Right, Lizard, although if it were Diamanta…," Spider's voice trailed off.

Esmeralda dove in and tried to rescue the "Savvy creature" who, it turned out, did not want the game to end and spun and wiggled in such a way that she could not be held onto. Eventually Esmeralda swam to the dock where Julieanne and Maxine sat watching in amusement. The smell of algae, a smell that could be bothersome, suddenly seemed pleasurable as the reeds swayed ever so slightly in the warm breeze.

"We'll make a swimmer out of you yet. You'll be in great shape by the end of this summer," said Julieanne.

"Hey, I just wanted to warm up a second," Esmeralda grumbled as she dove back in and swam and treaded water with Savvy, who had been caught, then freed from her captors. She imitated Savvy's moves. Consequently, the water began to feel like air and Esmeralda felt as though she were flying instead of swimming. She wondered if the release and the freedom she felt were the same as what Savvy experienced in the water.

Eventually Esmeralda got to the point where she had to stop. She climbed onto the dock, but sat by herself, content to watch her otter-like friend swim through the reeds and to view the clown dives of the two boys. *Was freedom more a state of mind than body? Or were they equally important and worked in conjunction?* She wondered to herself.

The rest of the summer was filled with the glory of nature and the festival of activities it inspired. The group engaged in many more days of swimming, plus hiking, bird-watching, estuary explorations, ocean drop-ins and the occasional visit to Bill's "museum". Frequently Esmeralda and Savannah found a loonie or other money or some jewelry. Whenever this happened the girls gave each other a "thumbs up." This was Esmeralda's favourite signal, for Savannah had a unique way of swirling her thumb to the top of her hand, almost like a magician in the midst of distracting the audience. Esmeralda could not copy the movement.

As for the treasure finds, for a while Esmeralda, was suspicious that something odd was going on, but later decided that there was either some kind of "good luck" in their friendship or that they had become a perceptive duo. Spider came to visit his cousins three times, and once, Samuel returned home to Victoria with him, while no complaint came from Esmeralda.

The girls continued their storytelling sessions in the field, often accompanied by assorted melodies and rhythms. Sometimes Esmeralda just sat and smiled in wonder at how Savvy could recognize most songs on the radio long before the words began. She enjoyed singing along as Savvy found her own way of expressing her love of music—rolling her tongue to the rhythm, or singing "doos" and "dahs" the whole way through, or changing the words to make the meaning more fitting to her concrete world as in "Take it to the Liver" instead of "Take it to the Limit."

Their full days would often beg for a supper together and then a sleepover. Sometimes Esmeralda needed a break from her friend's repetitive motion and words and the loud and shrill excitement that often came with it; sometimes Savannah was too unpredictable, impish or destructive. But after a day, perhaps two, the girls returned to their playful partnership.

Esmeralda wondered how she should deal with her friend when Savannah got "wild" and whether it was her place to be the disciplinarian. She wanted so much to help her friend fit into the real world. *How would Savannah survive as an adult? Would there always be someone to keep an eye on her?* At the same time she could not remove all the wonderful qualities that made Savannah uniquely delightful and the way her bliss seemed to light up the world.

On Vancouver Island, one can almost picture a daring carnival being carried by the September air. Everything changes so quickly. The trampoline-like temperatures bounce dramatically from nippy nights to toasty days. The carousel of changing gusts brings new looks to the landscape. Even the crowd-pleasing colour of the sky seems a little different each day.

When the air holds still, as it sometimes does at the quiet of day's closing, one can almost hear the sound of a distant calliope and muffled laughter. All these delights signal the last chance to be part of summer, and the people of this almost-paradise respond with a strong burst of life before the timely autumn slow-down.

Then there are the sunsets, that drifting change of the backdrop between the hills from blue to peach to magenta, from cobalt plum and deep indigo to black, often accompanied by a teasing dance of the clouds, airbrushed over with something warm, unclear and blending. Esmeralda watched the arbutus trees change colour with the setting sun, moving through a vast array of red shades before becoming dark. She thought viewing the sunset was as close as she would ever get to having a "Savannah dream." Often Savvy came out and joined her for this display, but usually chitter-chattered about other things than the sunset.

It was with an especially vivid sunset that the girls said good-bye to this summer. Savvy would rise with the next sun to board the van with her family.

Morning came and Savvy gave a half-asleep Esmeralda the longest hug that anyone had ever given her. Slight giggles came from many closed smiling lips when Esmeralda tried to free herself. Finally the family departed with Savvy repeatedly saying: "Are you a fish out of water? Are you a fish out of water?"

CHAPTER SIX

THE SPHERE

The cosmos of school had returned from its brief recess. It was not too bad this year since at least it kept Esmeralda busy. She kept making new acquaintances, but no real close friends. One day she realized that she had not found any treasures other than pennies for quite some time. This made her wonder.

Just after her thirteenth birthday celebration, however, her parents broke some news that seemed unbelievable.

Her mother spoke first. “Since I initiated the idea, I think I should be the one to communicate this to you. We have decided to move to the Vancouver area. I want to go back to university there and finish my bachelor’s degree in hopes of someday becoming a meteorologist.”

“Why do you want to study meteors?” asked Esmeralda with a sour look.

“Actually, meteorologists study the weather,” answered Bill. “Atmospheric Science. It’s something that’s always interested her. And now we have enough money saved up so your mother can go back to her studies.”

“But what will happen to your store Dad? You said you could never leave it.”

“Stan will look after the store here and we’re going to open a new shop in Richmond. Be fairly similar. Actually, this is a step toward realizing my dream—that there will someday be a whole chain of ‘Town Pliers’ all across Canada.”

Esmeralda glared as though incredibly angry, but still could not hold back a snort of laughter when she envisioned a chain made out of pliers that extended for thousands of miles. “This is a joke, right? Besides, you'd have to change the name to 'The City Plier' and that doesn't work. Please tell me the truth."

"No, honey, it's not a joke. We're serious," Maxine said. "I will go to school part-time and help your father in the new store. I really need a change. Now that you're older I don't see a lot of you and I get lonely. And I need a challenge, too."

"But you can find challenges here!" Esmeralda yelled.

"But *this* is the right challenge for me. I am sorry if you're angry. We thought you'd like moving to a place where there are more people your age. Again, I am sorry. We will come back to visit."

Esmeralda stormed to her room, muttering under her breath. "They didn't even ask me. They didn't want to know what I think. They don't care." In her room she opened the top drawer of her dresser, found the turquoise earring, squeezed it and placed it in her pocket, saying, "This shouldn't have happened."

Christmas was approaching fast. Esmeralda spoke to Uncle Stan concerning her mixed feelings about seeing the Andreasons again. She remembered the great summer she had shared with Savvy, but wondered if this Christmas the girl would seem entranced again and as hard to talk to as she was for most of last Christmas. She told him how she dreaded having to tell her friend that she would be moving and how she did not feel in the mood to deal with Julieanne or Samuel again.

Stan offered no real solutions. "This Savvy—if she's not the winter type, then don't bother with her now. Just move cold turkey. Why tell people? Is there a purpose? So, you can say good-bye sixteen times? Esmeralda, nobody's dying. You've been living in one place too long."

Esmeralda responded, "Haven't you been living in the same space a long time? As in head-space," while walking away.

Then, causing disappointment to change to despair, Esmeralda came down with the flu just four days before Christmas and had to miss out on some of her favourite events. A hayride. Carolling with neighbours—about the only time she saw some of them. Snow laid on the ground, but could only be appreciated from inside. She got out her old Kidplay tent and set it up on top of her bed, grabbed a felt marker and wrote the word "jinxed" on its yellow nylon. Then she climbed inside and stayed hidden, answering only to such demands as a full bladder and occasional hunger.

Three days before Christmas the Andreasons arrived at their cottage in their mud-sprayed van. Shortly, Julieanne knocked on the Mrky's door. Bill answered and explained that Esmeralda and now Maxine had the flu, but hopefully they would be better right after Christmas. Julieanne said that they would come back on the twenty-seventh, before they started their long trek home.

It was a memorable Christmas for the Mrkys, but not because of fun or frivolity. By now Bill was sick too. As the family sat beside their undecorated cedar bough, which substituted for a tree, it took all of their energy to open their gifts. They hacked away and barked out "thank you's" and odd artificial compliments to each other, as if they had exchanged gifts of kitsch. Upon receiving a new mountain bike complete with a bright red helmet, Esmeralda quietly said, "This is exactly what I wanted a few weeks ago."

"That red will make you visible!" Bill pronounced between coughs.

They all returned to their bedrooms, Esmeralda tossing her tent from her bed, and spent most of the next two days there.

December twenty-seventh. Esmeralda woke up. She started to sit up. She attempted to move again. She tried to suppress the coughs, but still they came. But she was definitely getting better; she knew it. She slapped her cheeks to make them come to life. Her facial muscles tight, she practiced making expressions in the mirror; then she worked on her larynx, trying for different sounds, and eventually she made herself audible. It was ten o'clock.

She got dressed, went to the kitchen, found a box of chocolates and plunked two into her mouth, put on her boots and parka and headed out the door, leaving her parents behind to make unpleasant noises without her.

As she ambled through the snow-patched, muddy meadow, Esmeralda wondered why she let Julieanne intimidate her so. *Why was that woman so hard to talk to?* She decided to try an old trick she had heard about a couple of times—to imagine Julieanne in her underwear to make her seem less daunting. The idea was quickly discarded, for she could not imagine what kind of underwear a shark-woman would wear, if any.

Instead she visualized a photograph of Julieanne on which someone had drawn a mustache and beard, rosy glasses, and a big fat stogy that just hung from her bottom lip. Many different hats she tried on her imaginary victim, but she had trouble finding one that fit. Finally, she chose a hennin—a long tube with a veil flying out the end, the type that an English maiden would have worn in the 1400s. This image did not work either.

Then she remembered something Samuel had once said about how his mother prepared for the first visit from the social worker. Esmeralda visualized Julieanne muttering, "Social worker better not think we, the Andreasons, are inadequate. No better place for Savannah than here," as she ran around cleaning up, then deciding it was too clean, then strategically spreading toys around, next deciding it was overdone, so tidying. Within a short time books would be strewn across the kitchen floor. "No. Not realistic." she would say, and, with unbelievable speed, as though she were riding the crest of a tsunami, she cleaned again. Shortly, she would carefully place healthy snacks around the house, and on and on.

This scene worked. Picturing Julieanne's frenzy, Esmeralda started to giggle, then burst into a deeper laughter. She stopped to regain her composure before she got any closer to their home. Then she heard odd noises, like screaming, but it didn't sound like Savvy. She walked closer. The ranting got louder and was accompanied by banging and clanging. She could now understand some of what was being said:

"The audacity! The nerve! What kind of a medal does he want? He expects me to think he's a great man. A great man? Just because he relieves me once every blue heron in June? Excuse me mister, should I kiss your you-know-what now or when it's more convenient for you, seeing as you're so busy being the perfect father…"

Esmeralda started to turn away, but then decided to go ahead and check and make sure everyone was all right. Hesitantly approaching, raising a limp fist, she knocked quietly, half-hoping nobody would hear.

Silence suddenly hit the air as if a sound barrier had fallen in front of her. Esmeralda waited a couple minutes, then Julieanne answered the door with bright red eyes and a big smile scribbled on her face, "Hey, hello there Elmer! Nice green pants! You seem to like green; am I right?"

Esmeralda felt confused. *Who was this woman, really?* At this point she decided that this unpredictable master of deception would never again scare her. "Yes, I like green! I like all the colours as a matter of fact. So does Savvy, but I guess you knew that since you're her mom. Is she home?"

"No, you just missed her. She left on a hike with her

dad and brother and cousin Cordy about ten minutes ago. Have you ever met my brother's boy Cordy? From Duncan? He's a little seven-year-old cutie—reminds me of Samuel when he was young. I can't believe Sam is twelve now. I guess that means you're thirteen. Surprised that I knew? Anyway, I decided to stay behind and catch up on a few things—like acting deranged and demented. Don't worry, just a little joke. Am I ever glad to see you! How are you? How're your mom and dad? Your mom still studying the avifauna?"

Avifauna? thought Esmeralda, *I hope someday somebody tells her that it's okay to call them birds.* She paused, then screwed up her face and said, "Do you expect me to answer all those questions or just the most recent ones?"

"Start with your health, dear."

"I have a lot more energy today, but I'm still coughing. I came because this is my last chance to see Savvy for a long time. We're moving to the mainland. My parents have really gone crazy this time!"

"Well I'll have to have a good long talk with them and see if I can straighten them out. Come on into the kitchen and we'll gab while I tidy and you wait for Savannah. It sure is a treat to see your grin again."

A grin was not what Esmeralda had planned on wearing to this costume ball, but soon the scenery changed and her smile disappeared on its own. As she walked toward the kitchen, she noticed furniture out of place, chairs toppled over and magazines torn and spread all over the place. The finishing touch was what looked like a raisin pie upside-down and mushed across the kitchen floor.

"Can I help you with anything?" Her eyes showed a sudden concern for Savvy's free-spirited mother.

Julieanne looked straight at Esmeralda. Her eyes began to well up with tears. She turned away and released a deep breath, "No, that's okay, what I should do is put my feet up. It's hard for me to do—I've forgotten how. Do you know how to put yours up? Your feet. Maybe you could teach me."

Esmeralda walked over to the family room and sat on a couch upholstered in pastel paisleys of cotton. "This is comfortable," she sniffled, "try sitting here."

As Julieanne sat on the couch, she released a long moan and placed her feet on the coffee table. "It is okay if I put my feet on this table, isn't it?"

Esmeralda answered, sounding only a little cheeky, "It's fine with me; it's your house." She got up and found the phone book and some other large books and one by one placed them between Julieanne's feet and the table. "Tell me when they're the right height?"

Julieanne whispered, "Ideal!"

Esmeralda ordered, "No thinking allowed. I'll be right back!" She searched the cupboards and refrigerator, finding little to choose from, but managing to get together some graham crackers and peanuts, then heated up a half cup of apple juice and put a marshmallow on top. She brought these remedies to her patient.

Julieanne looked up, eyes swollen, and said, "Delectable!" She sat back and nibbled slowly.

"No worrying allowed. I'll be right back!" This time Esmeralda brought a blanket from the bedroom and carefully placed it over Julieanne. The shark-woman now looked like a Pekinese puppy. Or like she deserved a halo. Her face had taken on the colour and texture of whipped Jell-O—the pinkish kind, probably strawberry. Julieanne fell asleep.

Quietly slipping into the kitchen, Esmeralda played a new character herself and cleaned the floor and washed the dishes. *Was she following the proper routine?* she wondered. She never knew what this perceptive woman would comment on.

The door opened and the house was suddenly flooded with noise. Then Nils, Samuel and Cordy noticed Esmeralda pointing at Julieanne and they went silent. Savvy kept chanting—something about a hooty owl. Nils headed toward the bathroom. Samuel and Cordy went back outside. Throwing on her parka, Esmeralda took Savvy's hand and they followed the boys. Once outside, the two girls hugged and then Savvy scurried off to play a chasing game with the boys, annoying them with her high-pitched screams.

"Is that what you mean by 'going gonzo'?" asked Cordy.

Samuel spoke out of the corner of his mouth. "That's not really gonzo yet. She's 'stimming', I think. The word comes from 'stimulation'. Now just imagine an hour or two of that. Non-stop."

Esmeralda sat watching on a log, but before long arose and walked over to Savvy, put her hands on her friend's shoulders and softly said, "Savvy, listen, I'm too sick to hang around. I have to tell you that my family is moving to Vancouver. My parents say we'll come back to visit, but I don't know when. I want to get your Arizona address so I can write letters to you there. Let's get your dad to write it down for me."

The two headed back into the house. Savvy went over to the Christmas tree and stared. Esmeralda heard a door open. When she looked up she felt a deep chill, for before her stood a strapping, clean-shaven man with blonde hair combed back from his face. It took a few seconds for her to realize that it was Nils. Her wide-open eyes followed him as he walked past the girls, looked at his slumbering wife and whispered, "I am so sorry, kind lady." Shortly, he looked at Savannah and quietly said, "Weren't you two out playing?"

Esmeralda responded, "Yes, but we came in to get you to write down your Arizona address. We're moving to Vancouver."

Nils found a pencil and some paper and wrote something down, then handed her the paper. Esmeralda hoped she could get her friend's attention. "I have to go. Bye Savvy. I'll write you stories." Savvy said nothing, but as Esmeralda turned around she touched her hand. She carefully took an ornament off the tree, a large crystal bubble with an etched design that resembled lightning bolts coming down from a never-ending sky. Delicate. Powerful. She handed it to Esmeralda, then returned to staring at the tree.

"Go ahead and keep it," said Nils. "Remember Savannah."

Esmeralda took a long look at Savannah, then said a quiet, hoarse "Thank you," and shuffled toward the door. She stopped and reached her right hand into her pocket, took out the turquoise earring and walked over to Savannah. Gently she placed it in the girl's hand, guiding Savannah's fingers around the charm. Savannah used her other hand to swing a quick "thumbs up." Again Esmeralda shuffled, head down, toward the door.

Outside, as she started moving toward her home her attention was drawn to the two boys, who were now sitting on the log where she had previously sat. She decided to spy on them in revenge for the times that Samuel had done the same to her. Quietly, carefully, a mouser sneaking up on her prey, she hid behind the garry oaks, surreptitiously creeping, then darting from one knobby trunk to the next. When she got closer, she observed that Samuel and Cordy were both whittling with jackknives on small pieces of wood.

"I can't stand your sister. She is so strange. How can you stand to be around her so much? Doesn't it drive you crazy? Don't you just..."

Esmeralda shook her head and looked down. Listening to another pompous blonde boy definitely did not interest her, and besides, she was stifling a cough, so she started creeping quickly through the woody bog. Concentrating on not crunching the snow, she missed hearing Samuel's response:

"Well, if you knew my sister better you wouldn't say that. In fact, you would probably love her too. She is so nice! She's different from anybody else in this world."

Back home, Esmeralda made an effort to avoid her parents and glided straight into her room. Still holding the precious gift, she flopped onto her bed and proceeded to engage herself in that long-awaited coughing spell. Once the fit had subsided she examined the sphere, looking at it from different ranges and angles, standing on her tiptoes with wide-open eyes, like Savannah, for long periods.

Laying on her back, she held the sphere up above her eyes and squinted into it for a minute. She gazed even deeper into the sphere, searching for its absolute centerpoint. Then everything started to look fuzzy and she checked her forehead for fever. Presently, she felt entranced. She heard a faint music, an unclear sound, like many voices singing and countless instruments playing different songs at the same time. Images swirled by—horses, mirrors, stars, guitars, chocolate bars, water, bicycles, tigers, visitors from afar—an inexplicable assortment of objects all thrown together in a ubiquitous mosaic, everything everywhere, and then changing, with all the objects present in exactly the same spot at the same time.

"Welcome to Savannah's world!" Esmeralda gasped and then looked away.

PART TWO

CHAPTER SEVEN

THE CAROL

Despite Esmeralda's frequent protests, the move took place, happening in the spring. She no longer went by Elmer—that name would be reserved for Savannah's use only—even though, as she made quite clear to her parents, she doubted she would ever see her again. Entering a new school near the end of the year did not thrill her. She made no friends.

During the summer she had little to do since she knew nobody. Encouraging her to meet people was akin to forcing a loner of a lioness to join a pride. Her mother suggested she join a club or team, but Esmeralda said, "no point in it" and became growly and snarky. She would feel like an "inside-outsider," she complained. With her head low and her eyes intent, she exhibited a stalking-like posture as she rode her bike, and when she reached her destination, usually a park, she would sit in a tree and devour a book as if it were her prey. Then she would bound off again.

No cage held this teen. She spent a great many hours riding her bike through the plains of residential Vancouver, smirking at the mismatch of the dirt-stained stucco houses and the many replaced roofs of rich red clay. Riding along, she sensed herself becoming stronger with each turn of a pedal. She felt sadness and anger burning away as though a small sun had begun igniting within her. The warm air stroked her face and wiped away her tears, as though it were a secret guardian.

By the time she returned from her lengthy rides to

their rented green bungalow—why they had chosen the same colour of house as before, she had no idea—she had gained the strength to let the obnoxious comments of the inconsiderate neighbour children roll off her sweating back—comments like "There goes Little Red Riding Helmet."

With no hoopla, no hip-hoorays, no nervous insides or sad shudders summer came to an end.

When she returned to school, in grade nine this year, Esmeralda put little effort into her work and her marks suffered. *What was the use?* she wondered, believing she had lost the ability to think things through when she had parted with Savannah. She could no longer write or think up stories because here there was no audience that was truly interested. It seemed useless trying to make friends because she was so different from these tough-talking city kids who spoke of things she had never heard of. Worse, they made constant references to television shows or commercial jingles, and since Esmeralda had little interest in television—her family owned only an old portable with a fuzzy picture—she usually had trouble catching the jokes, and this made her feel stupid, even though she knew better.

When a teacher asked her if she had some pictures of her old home and friends, Esmeralda shyly said, "I'll ask," and shuffled away. Later, she did ask her incessantly studious mother, who she now referred to as "Meteor Woman," why their family lacked a camera.

"Well, I suppose I've never really felt like I needed one," Maxine responded. "I rely on my memory to bring back the past; take snapshots with my mind as things happen, do you suppose? Oh, that sounds pretty hokey doesn't it? Maybe I just live in the present these days. Or is it the future? And I don't worry much about the past. I guess your father must be the same way. I've never given it much thought. Strange for someone who will be analyzing satellite photos to not be interested in pictures, you must be thinking."

Esmeralda mused over whether her parents ever really gave anything much thought—anything important that is.

Before too long, unopened boxes of Christmas decor in the middle of the living room signaled the imminent arrival of the holiday season. Mid-December. Esmeralda felt drawn to the boxes as an almost forgotten feeling of curiosity overcame her.

Checking first that there was nobody around, she opened a box and glanced through it. Miniature trains, miniature tools and life-like birds—glass doves, porcelain seagulls and feathery cardinals, jays and chickadees—greeted her from their wrappings as if saying "Mrky Christmas!" She opened the next box, picked up a tissue-paper–wrapped ornament and peeked at it, then another and again another.

She started to put one back, but then drew it toward herself and unwrapped it further. It was her gift ornament from Savannah. She took the crystal sphere over to the couch and lay on her back and said, "Maybe you can help bring my friend and me back together."

She gazed into the ornament, as she had done before, and again it happened. Images fell from the lightning bolts. She heard the circus of sounds. Figures started to fall into a pattern, beautiful but complex. A few moments later she could hear just one song and see just one image, a snowflake, where before she had seen many. As she focused on the snowflake, Esmeralda heard young voices singing together like a choir, only echoing as if moving along a path like young monks chanting and strolling through a monastery:

Sing out young tones;
Winter comes here.
Ring out ethereal youth,
Show your own magic cheer.
Revel and celebrate,
Sounds of bells and laughter dissipate.
Love rings in spirit.
Wish they will hear it.
Joy that will touch their ears.

Quiet now young tones.
Into the solstice you peer.
Still feet daring youth,
For a moment absorb what you hear.
Sounds of warmth embrace sounds of snow.
The candle's flicker flirts the mistletoe.
You will have the say,
For our earth one day.
Please let peace be near.

Then Esmeralda heard a different musical sound take over from the choir. It seemed vaguely familiar, the solo, the soft clear vocalism that curled the gently rolling folk ballad, but she could not figure out where or when she had heard it before:

Come the long December night,
We will follow a calling light,
From the Pleiades—seven sisters of the sky.
Out of reach of Orion's anger;
Guiding us from beckoning danger.
Brother Aldebaran trails years behind.

Once their nebula squeezed to fiery roars,
As they lost all cold that lay in their cores.
Sister's warmth being brilliant, near ever-strong.
Frost-stung eyes see ice sculptures—palaces proud;

And popcorn puffs turn to heavenly clouds.
We're star-drawn, so we venture along.

In time snowflakes fall—white sisters themselves.
And they warm our hearts as we watch them melt,
As we know more will come to astound.
See sparkweed seed sown by gust throws;
Barely nourished by the softwater snows—
Blithe confetti of our common ground.

Grow to winter gardens, seeds—red, blue and green;
Mirror off icy soil—magnitudes unforeseen.
Growth keep reflecting; reaching up high.
A sheer of flying light wakes and pleases,
And signals the changing of the seasons;
Enchanting the seven sisters of the sky.

Dance, sisters, play,
By day in your chiffon fan dresses.
Powder your gleam.
Comb every beam.
Smart comments your brother expresses.

Swing, sisters, fly,
By night in your bold sequin dresses.
You are the stars;
The galaxy is yours.
On your light someone may be dependent.

Gaining the strength to sigh a reverent cry;
Frightened, not we, by fires in the sky;
Not torn by winds that warn of a storm.
But we must trek back to the village green;
Sift the swift-deepening crystalline;
And curl up by homemade candles until warm.

Blow farewell kisses to the sisters and Aldebaran,
And curl up by a candle until warm.

Esmeralda now found herself taken by the sight of a candle. She became absorbed in the flame's intensity and then all in the sphere glowed a yellow-orange. Inside the flame she saw a summer day and within that day she saw herself.

She became part of that day. She was riding her bike while wearing her infamous red helmet. She was pedalling hard. She realized she was part of a race. Others were catching up. She saw nobody in front of her—only a large banner across the road and people cheering. Her lungs stung with each breath. She sprinted for the finish. She crossed the line first, wheezing with exhaustion. Nobody came over to congratulate her, they just kept yelling, "Go! Keep going!"

Then she eyed a movement, a flicker of light that was Savvy yelling "Keep going Elmer!" The other finishers put their bicycles and helmets to the side, changed their shoes and started running. Then, as Savvy held out a prize—an earring of silver and blue—Esmeralda realized that she needed to finish her triathlon. She had already swum, although it was a faint memory, as if it happened eons ago. Now she had to decide whether or not to run. The sky was sizzling and she was spent.

Esmeralda came back to the couch with sweat dripping down her brow. "Oh, my, my! Questions—coming fast! Not a pretty problem for a tired brain. This head needs a good long shampoo. But, first, a letter to Savvy. Maybe this will all make sense to her."

CHAPTER EIGHT

VISITORS AT LAST

As many know, stories begin with a small thought, but often surprise the writer by rapidly expanding into something far from the first picture. A path far from any other investigated. Esmeralda based an eight-page story for Savannah on her triathlon. She included a snapshot of herself, which she had taken in the mirror, for she had received a camera for Christmas.

If she ever made any friends in her new neighborhood, she knew she would immediately take pictures of them. In the meantime she practiced her photographic skills on the local cats, dogs and squirrels, and sometimes even her mother and father.

Two months later she received a letter from Savvy:

Dear Elmer,

Thank you for my story. It was fun. I am eating and swimming. Send me more questions to my answers. I love you.

Love,

Savannah Andreason, age 15

With that response, Esmeralda sat down at a table and started a letter:

Dear Savvy,

I liked your letter. Now I know there lives a chance that we will meet again and things will somehow work out for the best.

As for sending you questions to your answers...let me think…

That was as far as she wrote. Then she pulled out her homework.

Over time Esmeralda's optimism faded, but only a little. School was slightly better than at first. Not great, however. Some of the other kids would say "hello" and act courteous toward her, but she had no real friends. She still existed in a different frame—a frame that would never make it into the yearbook. While it seemed that rainshowers, thunderstorms, sunbursts and rainbows came in and out of the lives of others, her puddle remained stagnant, and she even asked herself, "What kind of a mutated creature would grow in still water?" She pondered a moment, then lectured herself, "There must be more to concern myself with than me and where I stand beside others, but what?"

During the summer she rode her bike to more parks and gardens and other photogenic spots and took snapshots to remember them by. When she got home she would get off her bike and try to run, just to see if she could, but her jellyfish cycling legs just wobbled and the muscles tightened, and the attempts never lasted long. She continued reading and tried to write poems like the ones she came across in books, but knew they were in some way lacking, and always ended up throwing her words to a garbage can. At least her written words were tossed. Evidence destroyed.

Time passed. Autumn, then winter came. One particularly dark dank day Esmeralda stumbled into her mother setting up a particularly dark green hemlock tree. Could it be that time already? Esmeralda was so used to the Christmas displays in the stores by now she could almost see through them, and thus, had stopped thinking about Christmas. Now the same realization occurred to her as happened every year—that the day of holly and warmth really does arrive eventually. Her mother asked if she would like to help in decorating the tree. This brought an immediate "yes" answer from Esmeralda. It always had.

Maxine commented on how each ornament unwrapped seemed like a little memory found again and each deserved a moment of reverence. Esmeralda paid little attention until her mother unwrapped Savvy's crystal sphere. Suddenly, strongly and stunningly it beckoned Esmeralda, and she asked, "Do you mind if I have a look at that?"

"Of course I don't," Maxine responded. "That's the one from Savannah, isn't it? You really miss her don't you? I miss her too!"

Esmeralda took the sphere to her room. She needed complete quiet. As before she lay on her back and looked deeply into the vast space within the sphere. *Savvy wants more questions. What questions can I offer? Will I find them here?* She heard the same mystifying music and saw the same snowflake falling toward her. As the songs floated along, the snowflake gradually changed shape until it resembled, no, actually was, a large silver question mark. A figure travelled along the top of the question mark. Slowly it moved until it headed downward with amazing acceleration. Then it jumped into the period at the bottom with a big silver spray.

"We have splash-down." The sound came from two simultaneous voices—one high-pitched, one low. Out of the period climbed two characters dressed in yellow and blue space suits with yellow masks over their faces and blue L-shaped tanks and numerous hoses on their backs. One carried an extra suit, which held a K-shaped tank with a mask and some unidentified flying gadgets attached.

Straight up to Esmeralda the two characters walked, staring right at her with intense eyes. When they spoke she could make out four distinct sounds—two from each traveller. Each had a high and a low pitch, and the harmonies their utterances created left

Esmeralda hopefully warm and cautiously chilled at the same time.

As a continuation of the winter carol they recited a poem:

Greetings to you from Curveplane L!
We've come to save this planet from hell.
You will need your oxygen tank today,
Though in L bodies it creates quick decay.
So we wear masks that remove oxygen,
Since here we visit Curveplane K again.

As the eagle taught us you shall put on wings.
Ready for flight? We'll pull the strings.
This suit will protect you from heat or from cold,
From space regression or quickly growing old.
We'll take you to space, then to our extension.
To let you see beauty without repression.

Let us start with planets Saturn and Mars.
We will traverse back after three distant stars.
There's the other side of the moon—powdery fun!
Everyone sees it differently—next we'll move to the sun.
Let's dance the corona and step on a flare,
And let it shoot us back to Earth's L atmosphere.

Aurora borealis, it's been a short while!
Light menageries of bumbling beasts in groomed furry styles.
Open this book to the ocean blue-green.
Orcas' backward breeches wash playful puffins clean.
Now child be pulled as balmy currents unravel—
Up where salty sandpeople work and travel.

You don't hear much about the sandman—why?
Unknowingly he moves in the Curve L sky.

He has helpers now—the "Sandpeople Six,"
Each bear dreams in knapsacks of hypnotricks.
For there live too many sleepers for one weary man
To lull with those silvery specks he calls sand.

Now view the tenants of the L extension,
Greeting each other with a touching suggestion,
Of harmony—through our onerous handshake,
Behind the back—both parties participate.
And it shows our trust and it shows our desire
To love each other and ward off greed's fire.

And when we inhale anger, then we kersneeze,
To make our harsh feelings blow away on the
breeze.
Then we can mend with a clear passageway,
To another tomorrow, sponging off yesterday.
You've seen enough of our plane—it's back to K,
To investigate how in your space you face your
today.

Quite a popular curve you live in dear child—
Domestication abounds, destroying what's wild.
For progress has taken your people in directions,
That only consider each one's personal perfection.
Sight has been lost of a primitive structure.
Evolution out of kilter. Who was the disrupter?

Not to blame the babies or those who plant the
seeds,
The father who nurtures, the mother who feeds.
But it must change and now—this resource drain;
There are too many people for your plane to sustain.
Care well for precious tykes who make their way to K.
Pray not for mass production based on the whims of
rainy days.

Because our planes are not exactly the same,
You must find your own ways; must find your own brains.
Science for pleasure we'll barely criticize.
If a smile it brings we'll scarcely ostracize,
But if avarice is the carrot, that's fairly your demise.
Look around, please tell, what do you surmise?
Doleful people crying?
Some young and old dying?
Fearless people flying?
Fearful people hiding?
Many just surviving?

Unfair,
yes,
but,

There exist too many great things you might lose.
The baton's handed to all Ks, you must choose.
Your living room could be as free as ours,
If you'd slow the polluting, the bigotry, the wars.
Please give them this message from Curveplane L.
Help deliver this planet from hell.

Taking the oxygen tank off her back, Esmeralda looked at the visitors suspiciously. "Do you always speak in rhyme?"

The visitors stepped away in a docile fashion. "We speak in rhyme most of the time, but when we have something to say, we say it anyway."

Esmeralda ridiculed, "Well, I guess you don't have anything to say to me then."

"Perhaps you will be that inhalation of pure nitrogen, oxygen, argon and other gasses that your Curveplane needs. That did not rhyme—correction, this depends on how you define 'rhyme'."

Then the visitors jumped back into the spaceship in the silver period. *Weersch. Zoop*. And they were gone.

When Esmeralda came back she was surprised to find herself sitting at her schooldesk. She sensed her teacher, Mr. Lobe, as his voice echoed around the room and thumped her eardrums to awareness, "So, they said 'his heart was filled with avarice.' Does anyone know what 'avarice' means?"

Esmeralda looked straight at Mr. Lobe, her puzzled expression unwilting. He smirked and said, "Welcome back from Christmas break, Ms. Mrky."

Esmeralda responded out loud, but not to Mr. Lobe, "What a bunch of preaching. Besides, the orcas would eat the puffins, wouldn't they?"

Water. Ice. Snow. She began to remember snippets of a Christmas. But which one?

CHAPTER NINE

SHUFFLE THE SPAGHETTI AND STIR THE STALK

By spring Esmeralda had spiralled to a new personal low.

She had again lost her desire to write or to communicate in any way because she felt terribly confused. More than anything she wanted to write to Savvy, but she didn't know what kind of questions Savvy wanted to hear. She did not know what to think of those decked-out sanitized Q-Tips from Curveplane L. *What was Curveplane L? Was it real? Were they right? What did they mean? Those were not the questions Savvy wanted to hear; they couldn't be!* Esmeralda knew she had wished for something other than herself to be concerned about, but this was too much.

At last, some relief from this puzzle came. Her father approached her as on their couch she sat wearing an expression of boredom. For a moment he watched her as she tried to snap her toes as though they were fingers. His voice cracked the silence:

"Little Gem, how would you like to come with me on a trip back to Lake Cowichan this July? Your mom will run this new Town Plier for us for a couple days. We can stay with Stan. I'd sure like to see how the old store is holding up. The old homestead too."

"Yeah, I'll come. As long as we can do some things I want to do. This may sound selfish, but I want to swim in the lake again. And I want to visit Savvy, you know."

"Sure we can do those things. We can't spend all our time at the hardware store. That would be a drag!"

A drag? That tiny comment forced Esmeralda to look at her father and see him differently. *Could it be that he was not quite as narrow as she had thought?*

On July twelfth, Esmeralda and her father packed their pickup and headed for the Horseshoe Bay ferry terminal. It being warm enough to ride the whole voyage on the outside decks, Esmeralda let the breeze of the sea breathe in her hair and on her lips and between her teeth. Her father walked up, stood beside her, smiled, and said, "You look awake again." Looking straight into her eyes he added, "You don't think I worry?"

"I haven't ridden my bicycle since last summer. I wonder why?" Taking snapshots of the torn crepe-paper edges of the islands they passed, Esmeralda commented on how in just a short time she would be able to photograph her old home and Savvy.

Stan's house was always easy to spot—the front lawn decorated with the chainsaw sculptures he carved as a hobby. Upon summoning Stan, good cheer spread followed by reminiscing, a tour of Stan's wooden zoo, and kitchen table talk. Esmeralda participated in the conversation for awhile, but soon became fed-up with how Stan was so interested in what Bill had to say and only half-listened to her. Consequently, her mind drifted, and she eventually caught herself waking as her face followed her fist, which followed her elbow off the kitchen table.

"Slippery table, eh, Esmeralda?"

She looked at Stan, who only winked at her.

On July thirteenth, after a solid sleep at Stan's house and a two hour long visit at The Town Plier I, the two travellers rode over to their old home at Honeymoon Bay. On the way Esmeralda asked questions about her friend, not really expecting an answer. "Will she be the same? Will Savvy remember me?"

Bill said, "I doubt if she forgets much, and whether it shows or not, I'm sure she'll remember you."

When they arrived at their destination, the old Mrky

property, the house now appeared toy-like against the growing trees and bushes, but the smell of the summer blossoms was exactly the same as Esmeralda remembered. The smell of her childhood. Bill parked his pickup at the dome cabin and Esmeralda pounced out, not so much like a lioness now, but more like a rejuvenated cougar. She sprang to the cabin door, ready to claw. She knocked. There was no answer. Signs of abandonment stood out—cobwebs, piles of stale dust and debris blown up against the corners of the balcony.

"Let's hit the water, Gem, then maybe they'll show up."

"Might as well, Billislav." Esmeralda sighed.

Now the smell of algae took over, meddling more strongly with the wind than ever. With the waves lightly lapping the shore like the peaceful breath of a sleeping giant wistfully dreaming about a cloud, the water enticed Esmeralda to follow her fingertips off the end of the dry, foot-scorching dock into the welcoming cool. She tried again to swim like Savvy. She could come close, but knew that what she was experiencing was an imitation of freedom, not the true freedom Savvy had shown her.

She climbed back onto the dock and carefully collapsed onto a towel. She began to formulate questions—things she wanted to know about Savvy, life and the world and how it all fits together. She gazed through a gap in the trees at the field that had first brought the girls together. Unattended grass stood up like spears piercing the complacent air, just as it had three summers ago:

"Savvy, what would you like to do next?"

"Elmer cook up spaghetti!"

"How do we do that?"

Savvy grabbed Esmeralda's hand. They quickly shuffled around the field together, as if to stir the spa-

ghetti noodles. The grass-stalk noodles began to flatten and weaken from being trampled. Hot day. Anything could cook. In a corner they combined dirt-lump meatballs with seasonings of sage, marjoram and cloverleaf. They prepared fine sand to sprinkle on top of the finished product. Then the two young chefs lay down on their backs chewing on pieces of honeysuckle and soaking up the warmth and smelling the savory aroma of their concoction. Esmeralda was sure she really could smell something cooking and even taste the wonderful blend of flavours.

Later, when the girls entered Savvy's house they discovered a big silver pot of spicy-smelling tomato sauce simmering on the stove. Beside it stood Julieanne, deeply involved in a novel. She looked up with a start:

"Did you smell the sauce? Seems you two are always hungry. I suppose you figured it out, you rascal children. Yes, it's your favourite, Savannah—spaghetti. Now take an ice cream stick and stop your wild sniffing. Both of you." Julieanne always wore a huge crooked smile when she chided. "It's okay Elmer. Savannah knows I'm not displeased."

Esmeralda wondered.

Savvy turned to Esmeralda and with a twinkle in her eye she chirped, "You look as cute as a fish."

Esmeralda's thoughts came trickling back to the dock. She wondered how Savvy could be so fun-loving, so exciting and pleasure-seeking without being selfish or greedy. It seemed she never had to look far for her pleasure either. There was an availability to it almost everywhere. Savvy certainly did not suffer from comparisonitis or jealousy. She had this wonderful ability to live in the present and not worry or even think about what others thought about her. Still, Esmeralda wondered if she really would like to be like Savvy. She tried to concentrate on this question, but she could not make herself explore the deepest space of this perplexing quandary. It was too hard.

On her way back home, Esmeralda started once again to form a letter. This one she would send to Savvy:

Dear Savvy,

I am sending you questions— I hope these are to your answers. Please tell me the answers again. I am more forgetful than you.

1. Can you see and hear as well as you can smell?
2. Why do you change?
3. Are you as nice as I think you are?
4. What do you think about when you look at the Christmas tree?
5. Why is your memory so good?
6. Is your memory so good that it gets in the way?
7. How is school going?
8. Do you still visit the lake?
9. Do you still have the turquoise earring?
10. Do you have a picture of yourself you can send me?

Miss you!

Love,

Elmer (age 15)

CHAPTER TEN

A BITE OF SALT

As Esmeralda and her father rode the ferry back to Horseshoe Bay, the Andreasons boarded a ferry from a town outside Vancouver called Tsawwassen, for they were on their summertime journey to Cowichan Lake. A long trip from Arizona with many stops had brought them, and Julieanne was trying to remember how to relax. She found a place in a sunny spot on the ferry deck to stretch out. The sea smell pleased her and its salty taste soothed her. She closed her eyes and reflected upon the past year.

Am I being overly optimistic in believing that Savannah is showing growth? I can't really tell. Why can't I perceive things better? Why can't I perceive things as well as she does? People say she shows her autism less and less. Are they just saying that to be supportive? Wishful thinking? Am I wrong in expecting her to change? What am I putting her through?

Oh, be quiet and relax like you were doing, the conditions are ideal. Gosh, it is blissful here. I wonder if the melatonin is making a difference—maybe that's it. She's sleeping better. We've sure made friends at last with the other girls—sleepovers, friends' club, cross-country team. How much longer will I be able to run with the girls? Do they ever love her.

Am I too tough? She must try. I used to seem nicer than I actually was; now I'm so much kinder than they can see. How strong I am I finally know—next to nothing embarrasses me, but in some ways I'm still a girl. I can't grasp all those meetings with specialists that I think will be the last for awhile but aren't. They can't tell me much that helps, and I'm afraid I still know so little, but when they can help it is such a gift. All the damn letter writing, mostly futile, just to get some basic services. Hoop-jumper extraordinaire—I move the playing pieces because I have to.

Yet, Savannah's smile is worth it all. And her presence. How could I not love her? Just think, a few years back, when she first entered adolescence, I didn't think I could hack it anymore; she could become so demonic, so angry at the world, so frustrated. She did make it through that phase though, now I realize it, and she's a wonderful wonder again.

Julieanne remembered how her children had played together so peacefully last winter as they constructed a giant "baked Alaska" in the snow. She shivered so slightly, then, at last, her body and mind melted simultaneously.

CHAPTER ELEVEN

CRIMES OF CHOCOLATE

November. Grade eleven.

Back at school Esmeralda plodded along through each dull day as though she carried a pack of bricks instead of books. She wasn't sure why, but she completed most of her schoolwork, and more quickly than before. Still, as much as possible, she avoided interacting with all those faces—many of them too happy, many flawless, many blank and non-communicative.

Most days she crossed paths in the hall with Garyd Nichols, an outgoing, boisterous boy in her grade. She often thought to herself, *Look how he walks, just like society adores him. He must think he's incredibly cute with his white curls and blue eyes. I don't think he looks all that great: bug eyes, pointy beak, no chin. I don't suppose most of these people can see past the curls though. He ogles at and talks to all the girls except me. How does he know that he's too good for me when he's never spoken to me?*

One day, just as she was thinking almost exactly that, Garyd swaggered straight toward her and shouted, "Hey, you're Esmeralda Mrky, aren't you?"

"I'm surprised you knew my name."

"Hey, everyone knows that name. And I don't mind asking if you would like to go out to a movie with me sometime?" He put his weight on one foot and leaned into a locker.

Esmeralda stiffened, glanced around, stuttered and shrugged her shoulders all at the same time; out trembled a "yes."

"Okay, just checking. I'll just tally that up on my scorecard. I'm up to thirty-four 'yeahs' now."

Esmeralda stood openmouthed. How could she be

so stupid? How could he be so insensitive?

"You can't be surprised at that number can you?" said Garyd.

From around the corner appeared two of Garyd's notorious group—The Planaria (named after that free-living flatworm) Gang as they were known around the school—Jayson Woo and Carmela Popkin.

Carmela yelled, "Zerve, Garyd Nichols, you aren't being a complete bonehead again are you? I hope you aren't doing your idiotic tally." Carmela's almond eyes squinted to challenge.

"Hey, Garyd," Jayson said in his Chinese accent, "I thought you'd outgrown that childish game. I don't know why we put up with him sometimes." He turned to Esmeralda. "Don't pay attention to him. He's a turtle-poser. He has no self-confidence."

Garyd said nothing as he put on a cringe, wince and grimace display.

In her deep mellifluous tone Carmela spoke, "Zerve, Esmeralda Mrky, that's your label isn't it? Do you want to scoot with us after school? We're hitchhoppin' to the Funky Quarter. Ever hear of it? It's downtown, kind of, near Granville Island. My Uncle Zigzag and his forever fiancée Lucy own it."

"No thanks," replied Esmeralda.

"Oh, come on Esmeralda Mrky, don't be a cynic on food. They've got great health snacks. And then there's the chocolate." Carmela wiggled her eyebrows, then turned to Garyd. "Yeah, you can come too, poser."

The mention of chocolate made Esmeralda think again. Carmela's chestnut hair suddenly looked like thick streams of chocolate sauce. She phoned her father, and he volunteered to drive the group since he had a few supplies to shop for anyway.

After school they all squeezed into the two rows in Bill's rickety pickup. Garyd's twin sister, Miranda, who was Carmela's best friend and a lifetime member of the body-piercing fringe, also came along. Esmeralda felt honoured and repulsed at the same time to be pressed against people she had always thought of as flaky yet scary. As she held her uneasy smile in place her mouth got sore, then numb in one corner, but the chattier members of the group commented on how it really had taken no time to get to the Funky Quarter.

As they entered the restaurant they were bombarded by the smell of sandalwood incense, which, with one more step, competed with sweet, savory and pungent aromas from curries and vegetarian chili, cornbread and eggplant parmigiana.

"It's good that each smell doesn't have its own freak-wild-loud colour that it could be recognized by." said Miranda.

Carmela added, "Yeah, we'd be zervin' those wafts twist and blend in swirling cyclones."

"How would a person find the way through? We'd be stupefied by those bending images," said Jayson.

Garyd joined in, "Yeah, we'd be lost by now."

African music lifted many an ear and Esmeralda could no longer walk in her usual manner, but she fit in, for the others had also gained a certain lightness. Worn, dented antique furniture rested on what looked like a mahogany floor, complete with scuff marks. The fifteen or so tables were covered with homemade cloths, each made of a different fabric, and embellished with baskets of non-matching dried flowers. Several shelves had miniature elephants on them, some of them incense or toothpick holders.

The walls wore framed posters—a melting pot of musicians—some folkies, some rockers, some jazz people. One poster, unframed with curling corners, of Jimi Hendrix stood out, seeming to beckon her. It was directly below the cash register. Behind the register stood a short man with dark curly hair and a handlebar mustache, yelling across the room to one of the customers:

"Dear Mr. Wintergreen, I still say it is the most elegant thing. Yes, scraped, no, shaved into the thinnest, frailest curls. My joy—I would marry it if I could. Forget Lucy. As you sit there in your windowed corner, do you not see the beauty of chocolate—its colour, its grain, its many textures." He had a strong accent, but as to its origin Esmeralda had no guess, except maybe Irish or Italian.

A plump woman slid out from behind the kitchen door. "I heard that, Ziggy. I owe you another one." Her frizzy heap of hair slowly bobbed with her back into the kitchen.

The only customer, other than the five teenagers, was a dark man, probably of African descent, with greying hair and a slight accent. He responded to the chocolate question. "Stunning packages don't always hold the best gifts. Sometimes they do. You have to experience what's inside to know. Let that remain with you, children." He laughed in one deep blast. "Hoh, honestly, I don't care how it looks Zig, not when it comes to this; this stuff tastes cosmic! I'd better have another. Gotta put on weight, you know. It's that time of the year." Esmeralda cocked her head and looked at Carmela as if to ask why this average-sized man would want to put on weight.

"Some people have no sense of aesthetics," mumbled Zigzag. Then he yelled in glee, "Hey, look it's my little niecie. Tell me child, is anything prettier than your uncle's dessert creations?" Apparently Zigzag had not realized that Carmela was no longer "little." In fact, she was almost six feet tall and quite big-boned.

"I don't want to crisscross that again, Uncle Zig. We just wanted to see you and Lucy Luby and get some eats. Let's grab that big table." She pointed to a table near the center of the place.

As they sat down Esmeralda asked, "How did this place get the name 'The Funky Quarter' anyway?"

"Don't you know?" responded Miranda in a superior monotone. "It's because only the funkiest one-fourth of the population will eat in such a place." She piled her long strawberry-blonde hair on her head, apparently trying to achieve the look, whatever "the look" was. Esmeralda wondered if that was Miranda's real hair colour; she was known to change it as often as she changed her name, which must have been every three or four months, and seldom did her hair look as natural a tint as it did this time.

"No show, Miranda." Jayson's big straight-toothed smile took centre stage. "It's called the Funky Quarter 'cause it's in the funkiest part of town, eh? Just look at all the music joints in the area."

Carmela put in her opinion. "Zerve, back in the late seventies when Uncle Zig opened this place he only charged a quarter for coffee. Pretty lean, huh? It was one funky quarter if you could get a bottomless coffee for it. Agreed?"

Zigzag was now hovering overhead.

"So, Zigzag, be honest, how did the restaurant really get its label?" asked Garyd.

"Hey, no goofy reasons. What ridiculousness! It just sounded good. Hey, the customers, they like it. Judging by my customers now, I should have called it the 'Monkey Quarter'. It's as though I'm looking down through one crazy monkey puzzle tree. So what do you order, my little mandrills?"

Esmeralda looked around. The others seemed unfazed by his comment. She looked back at Zigzag and suddenly blurted out, "I, um, can tell you have an accent. I just have to ask. No, I shouldn't. Oh, well, where are you from?"

"Canada!" answered Zigzag proudly. "But I always say an accent accents the food." He laughed. "And nothing wrong with asking. You are sincere."

The whole group, except Esmeralda, ordered a

health shake with yogurt and fruit and ginkgo, ginseng and a few "miracle" herbs thrown in.

"Yes, my brain says they are better than a banana split," said the lofty Garyd. "Hey, Zigzag, do the shakes really make you smarter?"

"Doesn't seem that way to me. You simians are the only ones who keep ordering them. My other customers say they taste 'noxious' or 'obnoxious' or just plain 'awful'."

Esmeralda decided to order the "Craver's Paradise".

"What's the matter, Esmeralda Mrky?" teased Carmela. "Is it chocolate time?"

Esmeralda was not exactly sure what she meant, so attended to her dessert.

When she got home, Esmeralda headed straight for the storage closet, found a box marked *FRAGILE* and opened it on the spot. After a short search she came across the carol sphere (as she now called it) and proceeded to carry it to the living room. Enroute she stopped at the kitchen to heist a plateful of the rich-smelling goodies her mother had just baked to put in the freezer in early preparation for Christmas. As she sat on the couch with fudge in her left hand and the sphere in her right, Esmeralda whispered, "It's still four weeks until Christmas, but today doesn't make any sense. I don't think you can help, but we can try anyway. Thoughts, where are you hiding? I know you are in me, but where? Come out and play with me today. Help me say or do something different and new. Sphere, can you help?"

As usual, Esmeralda saw the myriad in motion and heard the perplexing sounds; then she heard the carol, which was shortly interrupted by some alien troubadours singing out of key:

What kind of alchemy has taken place
To make a plain bean so rare?
Look, no myth, just brace your face (a two-way chase),
As it pulls you by your nails, teeth and hair.

Once a moon, fragrant demons put on a show,
As they come in a crusty brown boat.
Orders to entice you must come from below.
Where is your angelfood antidote?

Reality—a pantomime?
What drifts here? A chocolate crime?

Now you're hiding like a sea hag in a sunken stern,
So no one will see you dare play,
This game of deceit, decadence and yearn.
Gone's all innocence gained yesterday.

Still this tempting concoction keeps grabbing your soul,
Claiming to release fiends within.
But inventing a huge fiend that fits in the hole,
Of emptiness created by sin.

Is it a crime or shame?
A possessive endless game?

Beware this bittersweet brute can take many forms,
(And hide in the shallowest dish.)
Fire up baking chocolate—Samba Brownies perform,
With truffles and Dark Evening's Kiss.

Oblivion, fondue, chocolate chips, chocolate milk,
Mississippi Mud, Marble Trouble Toiler.
Sauce spins over pretzels, a fine syrup silk,

Spooned out from your white double boiler.

Consider an exasperating festival.
A rocky road for those cocoa cannibals.

Now your log raft wrecks sliding a muddy shoal;
As a sea rat you scurry up the mast,
And you see you're being laughed at by a hideous troll—
Both unaware that like your craft he's melting fast.

Don't be fooled by names like Heavenly Hash,
It's Satan's food all the same.
And "Gift of the Gods"—a misnomer, how brash!
A contradiction wrought with false fame.
Call it the devil's divinity.
Call it the demon's delight.
Say what you may; say it weak,
Your tongue gliding in your cheek.
'Cause chocolate's most always in sight.

In a voracious manner, Esmeralda now looked into a giant fondue pot filled with cubes of melting chocolate. The closer her nose got to the pot, the more sensational was the smell. The next thing she knew she was falling in, not as her old self, but as a peppermint stick of red, green and white. With no arms she could grab nothing and she did so want to climb to the top of the slippery chocolate cubes and get out before it boiled or cooled and hardened, cementing her in—but how?

As she wriggled she perceived the warm melting chocolate churning in a vortex around her and she felt a stretching of her legs, as though she were being pulled down a drain. Sudden laughter caught her attention, a terrifying sound that could have been from demons or trolls. Presently, she heard several voices speak in unison between their fits of laughter:

We're here from that Curveplane L,
With no reason to save this planet from hell.
Hey, we represent branch thirty-one.
We differ from eighteen—we just have fun.

Care? Who us? About anything but pleasure?
When we are gone won't matter how we measure.
Don't care what's on rotting tombstones tomorrow.
Will they write, hah! 'Didn't return what he borrowed?'

Branch eighteen will preach to find a way
To save Planet Earth from hunger and decay.
But I can't feel you nor you feel me.
We're as independent as individuals can be.

So when we're gone makes nil nada difference;
We'd better laugh now at your morose existence.
How numbskulls take earth so seriously.
How they sweat to get on trajectory.
Gemmy, there's no chance for that tethered sea!

So take this message from Curveplane L.
You've no hope of saving this planet from hell.

A bitter stale taste soured Esmeralda. She gave off a sweet, but putrid odor. Feeling like a stuffed mousse, she wanted to loosen the belt on her jeans, but had trouble with her dexterity. She held up her hands. They were covered in a brown stickiness. She inspected her clothes—brown-streaked and grimy. And the couch—tastefully decorated? Subsequently her fingers rubbed a flakiness from her face.

Looking into the mirror, she laughed like her latest visitors. As she washed her face, she smirked and said, "Oh well, at least I'm glad chocolate is my only addiction! Maybe something interesting will come of all that has happened, although what I definitely do not know." She felt like running around the block to get rid of the dead, bloated feeling inside her, but instead succumbed to a sudden urge to write to Savvy. She had not heard back from her friend since she had sent the list of questions. Maybe an unconventional story would elicit a response.

CHAPTER TWELVE

NAMASTE

Another school year came to a close, catching Esmeralda by surprise because, unlike other years, this spring had managed to avoid dragging itself out to a new definition of endlessness. This year she had a few people to talk to in the halls.

And there was Carmela. With the freedom of no school and little responsibility, Carmela spent a great deal of time around Esmeralda, often meeting her at a park or beach. On one of the most prime of summer days, Esmeralda used Carmela and "Desdemona Gravity Defier", Carmela's Alaskan Malamute puppy, as photo subjects. The two young women ended up having a lengthy conversation about friendships. Esmeralda said, "I guess we've hung out together long enough that I can ask you this: Why is it that you decided to become friends with me anyway?"

"Hey, I like anyone with a strange name. You're talking to a mascara maiden who plans on going through her whole life as Carmela Popkin. Zerve, I'm not like Willow, the former Candace, the former Miranda, etcetera, etcetera. She's so worried about her label that she has to go around changing it all the time—hair colour matching the name but not the face, and clothes not matching each other unless they contrast the hair and jewelry. Socks and undies should never match anything, though. Got it?"

"Yow!"

"It doesn't matter if things like piercing or hair dying are in or out. Miranda declares that in her world what is 'in' is 'in' forever. I want to believe her."

"Why?"

"I wish I could believe everybody."

"But you, Carmela, could enjoy the pleasant surprises that come with being a skeptic who is often wrong."

"No, not in my world. I'm only the occasional skeptic. That's your world where skepticism is fashionable."

"I wouldn't call it fashionable. It's a need, a requirement, an urge. Is it an addiction? I'm skeptical of that, but whatever it is I will keep it under control for now, 'cause more important to me, I want to know who Willow started out as."

"I promised her I wouldn't tell anyone. I first met her in grade three and right away we became friends. Girl-be-dowdy, her name was bizarro! Her hair, too, the wildest shade of blue."

"Somehow that doesn't surprise me. How about Jayson? His name isn't weird, but he's still your friend."

"Jayson Woo? No, I suppose his Canadian name isn't, and I can't remember his Chinese name, but he himself is—weird that is. Is he ever! Who else would have the nerve to stumble into Mr. Kimball's class ten minutes late with that old dented tin coffee pot in one hand and his chipped red mug in the other, along with all his papers? Did you hear how he was trying to keep from dropping his turn-in and ended up pouring half the japing pot on it by mistake? Bites his lip. It's bleeding. He immediately turns to get paper towels and runs right into, you guessed it, the half-open door. He's as klutzy as Willow Nichols. She gets away with it somehow... Do you remember when she wore all that heavy multi-coloured eye shadow all around her eyes? Guess what happened there. Could she have fallen into a shelf in the library? Well, anyway with Jayson, his accident happened several weeks ago and he still has a mark on his knockin' forehead. What a frobe. I like that guy."

"Do you mean like or *like*?"

Carmela answered, "Like," with no revealing

expression. "What did you think?"

"Like *like*—like in *like*." Esmeralda played along, discarding the urge to be more intrusive.

Bike rides to Stanley Park or Jericho Beach for a swim and the occasional excursion to The Funky Quarter with Carmela and her group filled the rest of Esmeralda's summer. She found it ironic that she hung out with the Planarias, being that she despised their feigned worldliness, but they were the only ones to befriend her since moving, and they were probably better than nothing. At times.

On their final visit to the restaurant before the start of grade twelve, the group ended up having a lengthy discussion about holistic medicine. Esmeralda felt naive about such things next to the others, particularly the former Willow, now Fiona, who currently sported rustic browner-than-brown hair that matched her painted but chipping fingernails. Carmela also had deep brown nails. Supposedly this was to symbolize their 'connectedness' to the earth. Esmeralda wondered, to amuse herself, why they didn't just dig around in the ground, even work a garden, to get their nails looking earthy.

"Have you ever caught how Zigzag and Lucy never change the decor of this spot?" exclaimed Garyd. "Let's ask him about it. Hey, Zigzag. Come here."

"Are you misfits ready to order at last?" asked the jovial Zigzag.

"I wish we were," said Jayson. "0.06 Earth gravities on one chair. Know what I mean?"

"You're not ready." Zigzag shook his head and put his pen and pad in his pocket.

Garyd spoke up. "No. Actually, we were all wondering why you still decorate this place like it's straight out of the sixties? Just look at those, what do you call them, tapestries? Don't they look a little outdated to you?" The meaning of 'tact' was something the rest of the group had discussed and considered explaining to Garyd on several occasions, but each time had ended up concluding that if they did, they might as well also catch a porcupine and adorn it with bows.

"Hey, where did you children extricate this fungus from anyway?" said Zigzag. "Listen, child, don't rile me. People come here. The food is good. The conversation is good. Look, there's Mr. Wintergreen telling stories to those children. We call his table the story corner. See? And, this is not meant to look like the sixties. And, besides, look on that wall. Just look, I've got Smashmouth and The Hip, and there's Sarah and The Verves. They're not sixties, they're nineties and beyond—big big diff, Pluto. There are the Crows Counting the Cranberries. Hah! I put in what I like. This is not a place for trendy people and I won't change the name either, so don't bring that up. This is for people who want to enjoy their meal."

Garyd whispered to his sister, "The Verve isn't sixties? Fooled me, I guess. You know, I think he's too cheap to redecorate."

"Oh, go back to your virtual reality, Garyd Nichols," Fiona responded. "Or I guess maybe that's where your head is already." She used a long brown fingernail to poke one of his curls.

"More like virtual fantasy!" said Carmela.

"So, tell me, what have those of you who are not rude been doing?" asked Zigzag, his forehead freshly plowed.

Nobody answered.

Finally, Esmeralda spoke. "We've been making plans for things we can do after school once it starts up again."

"Oh, like get a job?" inquired Zigzag. "I could use some help around here. Business picking up!"

"Well," Carmela said, "we actually were considering

such interterrestrial ventures as studying homeopathy, acupuncture, aromatherapy, reflexology, ayurveda, and what else Fiona of the Nichols?"

"What happened to your foray into the field of yoga?" asked Jayson. "I planned on joining your class this year." He smiled at Carmela.

"Oh yeah, we wouldn't forget yoga. There's a Yoga for Teens class at the Rec Centre. Do you wanta come, Esmeralda M.? There's no way that Garyd will come."

"You are right on that one! Now that is virtual fantasy," said Garyd. "Besides, I'll be trying out for the hoops team."

"Of all the ideas mentioned so far, yoga sounds the most interesting," drawled Esmeralda. "What kinds of things do you do in your class?"

Fiona started to answer, "Oh, we do *asanas*—poses, that is—and breathing and—"

She was interrupted by Jayson, "I hear that they actually spend most of their time doing that 'yogic flying' thing. You know, where they pretzel themselves up in the lotus position and bounce around on springy mats to try to save the world. And I'm going to do that too. You'll see."

Zigzag insisted that they order now, and several minutes later he brought their food. After a manicotti healthwich and a yantra mantra pepper-lemon tea, Esmeralda noticed it was time to catch a bus home. The rest decided to stay behind and hash around their plans awhile.

As she was leaving, Jayson and Garyd put their palms together as if praying, looked at Esmeralda, bowed slightly and said, "Namaste!"

Putting her hands together, Esmeralda echoed them, hoping that what she was doing did not have some unwanted meaning.

Zigzag discarded his accent for several seconds, "We really do need more people waiting tables,

Esmeralda. No joshing! Business has improved and Lucy's overworked—needs a break. That means I'll have to do more in the kitchen."

On the bus ride home, Esmeralda thought a little about waitressing, but mostly about the notion of taking yoga. Maybe it was time to pick up a new interest. Still, she needed a clearer idea of what this "yoga" was all about.

Even though it was early September, when she arrived home she got out the carol sphere. She took it to her room, sat cross-legged on the floor and became engulfed in its images. The carol sounded prettier than ever, then started sounding exotic, possibly East Indian in nature. Suddenly she found herself in the middle of a large room with a spongy blue mat covering the entire floor. Cloaked in white gauze were ten or so people, including herself, all skillfully bent into the lotus position, some bouncing lightly and all concentrating deeply—hands resting on the knees, eyes closed. *Relax, relax, breathe*, she slowly repeated inside her head, similar to the way Julieanne had done for Savannah when they left the gift shop in Chemainus.

Esmeralda found the pose less difficult than she expected. She opened her eyes and realized she was starting to wiggle up and down without any effort. A large, odd and elaborate thermometer marked with labeled pictures of planets decorated the wall in front of her. She studied it, trying to read its detailed markings. Soon she found herself bouncing and she felt the corners of her mouth gradually lift with each new height. Now the floor moved like a trampoline. Higher. She watched the thermometer's needle drop down toward a small circle marked "Pluto". Was the room cooling toward Pluto's temperature? It didn't seem so. Higher. Higher. She was landing softer, but rising higher. She looked at the meter again and observed that at the top it said

GRAVIMETER. The room was almost to Pluto's relatively slight gravity, she realized. She closed her eyes, wondering what it would be like to have even less gravity.

Higher. Higher. Higher. Now the height she reached scared her. She opened her eyes again, just in time to see that she was about to hit the ceiling. However, a fraction of a second before her head banged, a small hole appeared in the ceiling, and she straightened her body just in time to slip through it and beyond into a clear blue sky. She crinkled her face as she anticipated the long fall and landing, but just as she started to descend she gently alit on something soft and furry.

Could it really...a flying tiger? A winged tiger! While travelling at a remarkable speed, maybe as fast as a jet, Esmeralda stared at this magnificent creature. It looked like pictures of tigers she had seen, with, of course, the exception of its wings, which were shaped similar to a bird's but colour-patterned much like a monarch butterfly's, and fuzzy like pilled velveteen. The regal animal carried a large canvas bag around its neck. It spoke in a deep, muffled, almost cartoonish plea:

"Oh, dear, I am afraid I really must be lost, and if I land now I may not have the energy to get back up here again. My sweet young lady, I'm assuming I have chosen the right language to speak to you in, would you please take the bag off my neck and get out the camera. It has the zoom lens on already and you can use it to help guide me along. Oh, would you? Feel free to take pictures of any points of interest, but not yet, not to the right anyway, those clearcuts are like scabs on my eyes. It's okay now, we're past them."

At last, here was something Esmeralda had no trouble handling—a camera. She used the zoom lens to make out what she believed was the Puget Sound up ahead.

"So, I think by the looks of things we're heading for Seattle, but where is it that you want to go?" she said.

"I do so want to return to my jungle home in India. Come with me. I will take excellent care of you there. You would make a wonderful jungle child. Do you know how to get there? I've been lost for hours."

"Well, I believe India is next to China so let's try this," she suggested, recalling something from her days with Savannah. "Take a left turn at Portland. I'll watch for it."

A short time later they were over downtown Portland. "Left? Good! All right, now take a right turn at Scotland." As they travelled on, Esmeralda said, "I've never heard of a flying tiger before. How can you exist?"

"I always wanted to...hey, watch it! You're rubbing my wings the wrong direction." said the tiger. "That's better. Pet gently...I've always wanted to see things from a different point of view. I've always tried to look at things in various ways, but thought there were many more. One day, you see, I had been too deep in thought to get all the seeds out of my fur, and suddenly, these buds appeared on my back, and they just, hmm, blossomed into wings. Don't know why it happened."

In practically no time the two were flying faster than ever and right over the Atlantic Ocean. "Doesn't Earth look lovely from up here? It used to look even better," the tiger said.

Esmeralda confided, "I've seen the other side of the moon. Fantastic, eh?"

"Have you really? I am envious." said the tiger. "That is one thing that I've always wanted to do, but there is a slight oxygen problem out there. How did you do it?"

"Some oddball characters let me borrow an oxygen tank and took me there."

"And how did it look? Not that it would look the same to me, of course, because, from what I hear, everyone sees it differently."

"Well," answered Esmeralda, "it was fluffier than your wings, and colours seemed to look kind of different from the way they looked before, and a voice called from it only it said nothing and I couldn't hear it, but I knew it was peaceful all the same. That probably makes no sense, does it?"

"Always remember how you saw it," sighed the tiger.

Suddenly he slowed down and yelled, "There it is—the turquoise triangle—grab it! This may be your only chance."

Sure enough, hovering in the air was a triangle the size of a yield sign, made of silver and covered with turquoise stones. As they flew by, Esmeralda reached out to grab it and she toppled off the tiger. She managed to stretch her arms and grasp a hind leg just in time. Sailing by trailing from a tiger's paw, and a fast one at that, was a remarkable way to travel, but her arms were tiring. Struggling and grappling, somehow she managed to pull herself up onto his back. She had not touched the triangle, but she had gotten close enough to see that there was some kind of inscription on its side. Perhaps the inscription would have given them directions, perhaps not. The two persevered and took their right turn when they spotted the English Channel to the north, realizing that this was as close to Scotland's banks as they would get.

"All we need to do is take a left turn at majestic, a right turn at pizza and a left turn at the swimming pool." Esmeralda continued navigating and soon they turned above a set of majestic mountains, which the tiger decided were the Pyrenees. After hugging a coastline for a few minutes, they turned again over the boot-shaped peninsula that they recognized as Italy (Esmeralda always thought of pizza when she thought of Italy).

Halfway across the Mediterranean Sea, they figured that this must be the "swimming pool," and they turned left. A few breaths later Esmeralda suspected that they were over India. The air was still and silent and hot, yet fragrant, resembling the air within the Funky Quarter before opening time in summer. Ahead, just beyond a small lake, lay a thick jungle. It became noisy and noisier still, as though a multitude of excited creatures lived within the jungle's camouflage.

Esmeralda remembered something. "Uh-oh, I forgot the part about turning at Information. I'm sorry. I fluffed."

"What? It is hard to hear. Did you say what I think? What do you mean—fluffed? *Fluff* is not a mistake! No matter. Looky! There's my habby home up ahead! I recognize it. I invite you to stay with me. I would be delighted to have you." The tiger went into a steep descent.

Esmeralda decided to make a quick exit before they landed. If there was one thing she knew from her limited experience in watching cartoons as a youngster, it was that you should never accept invitations from overly friendly carnivorous creatures. "No thanks, but thanks for the ride," she said, returning the camera and bag to the tiger's neck. She dove off his back and plunged into the center of the lake. When she surfaced for air, she saw the tiger disappear between two banyan trees. All was silent.

Spotting a group of villagers on the shore, Esmeralda swam in their direction. Emerging from the lake, she felt a little embarrassed as the wet gauze clung tightly to her form. One by one, sightly people with dark skin, caring features and listening eyes walked up. Each one gave her a gift, then bowed "namaste" to her. The first, a woman, offered her a piece of blue towelling, slightly larger than a washcloth. The next, an elderly man, gave her a small red silk pouch. Those gifts were followed by these tidings: a miniature earthen water jug, a bumpy root about the size of her fist, and an amazing-looking purple and green striped flowering plant in a cloth bag of soil.

Esmeralda looked at the gifts and then at the generous people. "How curious that I'm so aware that I look different from the others here...even though nobody is treating me in a negative way," she whispered to herself as she picked a ball of tiger wing fuzz off her sleeve and placed it in the red pouch. Then she noticed thousands more people working away in the background. "I guess this is just a glimpse of what it's like to be a minority."

The elderly man stood in front of her. "I can speak English, do you?"

"Yes," replied Esmeralda.

"We see you caught a ride on the winged tiger. Not many can do that. Did you meet the turquoise triangle? Yes?"

Esmeralda nodded.

"To help you we have given you things you will need. You are so young now. Do not forget to use them before it is too late."

Another man spoke. "The rider of the winged tiger always has something important to say. What is your message?"

Esmeralda scratched her temple and paused, then said the first semblance of a message she could think of, "But it must change and now—this resource drain; there are too many people for your plane to sustain." She remembered the Curveplane L visitors saying that, then gave the villagers an apologetic look and said, "I can think of another message." The people said nothing.

At last, a woman spoke. "Truth alone triumphs. Go and fill your jug now. You may leave when you are ready, because you must miss your home. Do not forget to take your gifts with you. You will use them wisely. Sleep well, child."

Then the whole group said "namaste" to her and Esmeralda responded in kind. They slowly walked away. Esmeralda could not understand why she should fill her tiny jug—it would probably only hold a few drops. She took it to the lake anyway and dipped it under a ripple. The jug started to expand. She lifted it, looked inside and saw that it was empty, so she dipped it again, this time in deeper water. Now it grew at an accelerating pace and before she realized what was happening, it became much larger than Esmeralda herself. She hauled it out of the water and set it upright on the shore. Still, no water sat inside. By now she was too tired to think about how this made no sense.

Yawning and trudging along, dragging her jug, she looked for a sleeping spot, but the only shelter she saw was too distant. With her pouch of gifts around her neck, she ended up climbing, gingerly, into the jug's manhole-sized opening and curling herself in its warm spongy interior.

Just as she got comfortable, Esmeralda jerked as she perceived something scary happening. First, there was a back-and-forth grinding motion, then she started spinning around, first slowly, then faster and faster, as though she were on some wild new kind of amusement park attraction. The jug moved downward, as though it were a revolving elevator. She popped her head out of the top, and, by the increasing depth of the soil around her, could tell that indeed she and the jug were burrowing down into the earth.

Seeing no escape, she decided to just sit and enjoy the ride as much as she could, which was not a lot. *Is this the way home?* she wondered. As she went deeper it got moister, then hotter. When the heat became nearly unbearable, she noticed that the opening had shriveled to the size of a quarter, but heat continued pouring in as if from a blow dryer. In fact, the whole jug seemed to be getting smaller, which, of course, concerned her. She remembered the elderly man's words, "Do not forget to use them."

She took the root out of her pouch and used it like a cork, forcing it into the hole to keep out the heat. Then she pulled out the towelling to sit on as insulation. She stared at the flower, trying to think how she could use it. The elevator kept spinning, but was she going up or down? She couldn't tell. She stared at her gifts. *Were there other uses for them?* Within the spinning and grinding she kept hearing, "You will use them wisely, use them wisely, use them wisely." Soon she was asleep.

The phrase "Indian summer" would from now on bring extraordinary memories with it.

Over the course of the next week Esmeralda came to some conclusions. First, she (along with Carmela and Fiona) would try waitressing for Zigzag. Second, she would try one last time to reach Savannah with a letter. Third, she would not look into the carol sphere anymore unless she heard back from Savannah because it was just getting too strange and ridiculous—whatever it was that happened when she looked into its neverworld. Fourth, she would indeed try the yoga class, for she knew that it could not possibly be as bizarre as her so-visioned "visit to India." After what she had been through, she could easily handle a single yoga class.

The next Tuesday, Esmeralda clutched a blue blanket as she entered a small auditorium with Carmela, Jayson and Fiona. The instructor, a man of about thirty, asked them to find a spot on the floor and gently led them through some basic postures—tadasana, vrksasana, dandasana, baddha konasana (none of them the lotus position). He talked about breathing and encouraged them to lead with their hearts as though a pullstring were attached to their sternum. *Mildly weird*, thought Esmeralda, *but I have certainly seen weirder*.

After a few more asanas, a warming reached her sinews and they became vitalized as though many tiny harmless campfires had ignited throughout her body, all the way to the bones. An extinguisher of some sort reached her brain and she felt a soothing that was new to her. The stretching took effort. Of course. But no one complained (except for an occasional deadly grimace that burst through a sedate face now and then) because the benders and twisters of the world know the difference between a good stretch and warning pain, or maybe because others were doing their best to keep their tooth-marked lips shut. Peer pressure. So lives forgivable "pain"—once the pose was over, so was the discomfort. Truce declared, peace now appreciated, celebrated.

After the stretches they laid on their backs in savasana and let their bodies assimilate the work they had done. At the end, when all said "namaste," the instructor explained that in Sanskrit the salutation means something similar to "the divine in me greets the divine in you."

"This was fine—yoga, namaste and all," Esmeralda told her friends.

"Not too dorky, not too hard. Especially now that it's over," said Jayson.

"I suppose it wouldn't hurt for me to change my Western ways. Even if only a little," said Esmeralda.

"I need to change mine a lot," Jayson declared. "I think I'm less Asian than anyone."

CHAPTER THIRTEEN

THE WALTZING WAITRESSES

A year passed, and then another December came, signalling the time for Esmeralda to metamorphose into an eighteen-year-old. Continuously expressing her dismay that eighteen did not seem much different than seventeen, she started wearing her long red hair up in a sloppy bun, telling her friends, "something has to change." Actually though, three important events had occurred in the past year for her.

First, she had finished high school and started taking photography classes while still waitressing with Carmela and Bridget (the former Fiona) at the Funky, where business was bustling beyond the point where difficulty came in remembering the faces of customers. Bridget , expressing the "volcano-blown look" quite well with her standing flames of red, orange and yellow hair, worked fulltime. Carmela and Jayson were now enrolled at the University of British Columbia, and Garyd, with uncharacteristic sincerity, searched for a job.

Second, Maxine, after many unsuccessful attempts, had quit smoking.

The third event had happened the past summer. It was brought on by Jayson, who had burst into the restaurant one day with five tickets to a rock concert at Deer Lake Park Amphitheatre:

"Listen, gracious ladies, I want to take us all. Did you hear that Outrageously Normal is playing on the twenty-fifth? Brother's New-Fandangled Bungee Chords are opening for them. My treat 'cause I want to celebrate the fact that all us bozos have been glued since, well, for a long time."

"Admit it," responded Carmela, "your family is gruntin' rich."

"Come on, lay off, Carmela," snapped Jayson. "My family just has a nice house 'cause that's where my parents put all their money. This came out of the doughnuts I earned running errands. Don't you see I want to be nice, Carmela?"

"Sorry Jay! So who all is going?"

"You three ladies, of course, and Garyd and me. I'll pick you all up in my new Bug."

The girls looked at each other and screwed up their faces as Jayson walked out the door.

"Outrageously Normal? The Bungee Chords?" said Bridget, pushing a stick of beige lip-treatment in circles around her mouth. "No taste stranger than that boy's."

"It's the car ride that destroys me," said Carmela. "He calls it his *new* Volkswagen 'cause he hasn't had it long, but I've never ridden in anything so bouncy. Gosh, I hate this. That thing is so ancient. I can hurt his feelings on this one, can't I?"

"Is this one of those testosterone bands?" asked Esmeralda. "I don't really know them. No females on stage? None in the audience, except girlfriends?"

Miranda replied, "There is a lady drummer. If I remember correct-ally, she's the most masculine of the bunch. Ah, let's face it girls, we can't come up with any real good excuses. We'll have to go."

When the twenty-fifth of August came, Jayson arrived, smiling his huge grin behind the wheel of his red Bug. Esmeralda had never been to a rock concert before, but dared not mention this to the group. She wore a somewhat nervous look, but once the car got moving it turned into a terrified look as Jayson turned around on the lawn in front of Carmela's house and drove down the sidewalk until he found a break between parked cars so he could get onto the street. He had no reverse gear. Then, as they approached Deer Lake Park, Jayson was looking over his shoulder to say something to Carmela, who was in the back, when he accidentally pulled the steering wheel out of its socket.

His smile showed embarrassment as he managed to fit the wheel back in place. Garyd could not stop laughing. Esmeralda held her stomach with one hand and Bridget's shoulder with the other, for she knew in her gut-of-guts that the morbid soul of misfortune was planning its next horrid appearance.

Although the group arrived more than two hours early, they still could not get any closer than three-quarters of the way back from the stage. They sat on two blankets on the turf. A hodgepodge of interesting smells filled the air—some sweet, some unfamiliar, some both sweet and unfamiliar. Carmela broke out a bag of chocolate eclairs to share with her pals.

"What's the matter Carmela?" asked Bridget, "Is it—"

"Shut up, Bridget Nichols," snarled Carmela as she took a monstrous bite.

"So, you two, what's this I hear about a new religion you're forming. Is this for real?" asked Garyd.

"You bet it's real," said Bridget, "but it's not really a religion. Not in a traditional sort of way, anyway."

"It's a 'spirituality'," suggested Carmela.

"A spirituality, good girl, sounds like we know something! We call ourselves the 'Church of Good Hope'."

"I can't believe what I'm hearing!" said Jayson.

"Well, listen to this," said Bridget. "Why should people be bound into religions with all kinds of rules and customs that don't make much sense or aren't explained well? The common bond between most religions is the spirit of love and goodness. At least originally. In the Church of Good Hope, we don't want to take over from religion, we just want to bring people of different backgrounds together to share their kindness."

"Isn't that what we do in our group?" squeaked Jayson.

"Yes, but more people should be able to feel part of a cause for goodness," said Bridget.

"So, how does this 'cause' work?" Garyd said sarcastically.

Bridget never let her brother get the better of her. "Well, Garyd, this is how it works. It's amazingly simple. Anyone can join who wants to. All you have to do is be kind and worship whatever you want and let others do the same as long as they harm no one. Carmela and I have chosen to worship the spirit and wonder of the earth. We're working on our own handbook. We have a slight disagreement, though. Carmela seems to still believe that earth can be saved, so she wants that as part of our mission statement. I say we should just stay as healthy, mentally and physically, as we can until the earth dissolves into one little homeopathic granule."

Carmela breathed deeply in order to form her best expression of annoyance.

"That's okay though, right? If you two see it differently. Just have different mission statements!" said Garyd.

"Looks like we'll have to," said Carmela.

"Oh, and in case your curious minds are wondering," Bridget continued, "there are no dues and no meetings."

"But if people want to be spiritual shouldn't they get together to do so? To share their spirituality?" asked Jayson.

Bridget answered, "Oh, you can get together all you want. It's just not required. In fact, spiritual feelings can best be expressed through our togetherness—"

"What do you mean!" interrupted Carmela. "Being alone is sometimes necessary for ultimate soul development."

"True, now, we haven't come up with a good motto yet. Any ideas?"

Esmeralda tried to be witty, but, as usual, was taken for being serious. "How about 'the Father, the Son and the Holistic Ghost.'?"

"Hey, that's a good one!" stated Bridget.

Carmela added, "We might just use that one. You know, Esmeralda, you're a lot smarter than we sometimes give you credit for."

"No, just clever enough to fool people into thinking I'm smart," said Esmeralda with a nearly straight face.

"I could handle becoming best buds with my spirit, but I just don't want to hear, say ten years from now, that you two are leading some quirk-head cult—you know, getting rich off donations, separating families, living in underground tunnels as hypocritical self-proclaimed Messiahs, that kind of stuff." Jayson said.

Garyd kneeled with hands in the air, then bowed and chanted, "Hail Carmela. Hail Bridget, or whoever you will be."

As the rest of the group continued to talk about the Church of Good Hope, Esmeralda watched. She observed how Bridget kept her eyes on Jayson, how Jayson and Garyd paid particular attention to Carmela and how Carmela paid attention to everyone and everything. She wondered how, after so many years, this group had stayed platonic and whether that would ever change. The threat of AIDS undoubtedly had and probably would continue to make physical relationships progress slowly for many she knew, but what about such things as flirtation, infatuation, falling in love, boyfriends and girlfriends, abstained romance?

She closed her eyes and tried to picture herself in a romantic scene. She saw two people laughing together.

Who were they? She convinced herself to stop thinking about such things, for she felt that chances were not great that she would ever find someone who would truly love her.

She opened her eyes, saw Garyd and mumbled to herself, "If I do find someone, he definitely will not be a blonde."

Moving away from the talk momentarily, Bridget took an envelope out of her bag and handed it to Esmeralda. "Some guy left this for you at the restaurant. I'm assuming some kind of attraction from afar." She winked, then returned to the chat.

On the outside of the sealed envelope, it only said *Esmeralda Mrky*.

Inside Esmeralda found a brooch with a note pinned to it, which read, *A tip for you. From where music has no age. Are you spellbound?*

She looked at the brooch—a golden tree, like an oak. Set into its branches were four gems that looked like ruby, turquoise, emerald and diamond.

Thinking it a kind gift, yet not rock concert fare, she started to place the brooch in the small pocket of her daypack and said to Bridget, "I wish I knew who to thank. Or should I not? This is kind of creepy."

"Oh, you probably should. If I ever see the guy again I'll point him out to you. What is it he gave you? A brooch? Yeah, he did seem a bit old-fashioned. Any of them have significance?"

"Well, turquoise is my birthstone and Savvy and I once found a turquoise earring. That doesn't mean anything though."

"I'm amethyst—zodiac-wise that is. No purple gems there. Wonder if I'm on someone else's tree of mystery. Hmm, maybe the brooch is some kind of omen. Well, could be."

When the Bungee Chords ripped onto the stage all

conversation stopped. Esmeralda squinted, trying to focus on the far-off musicians. Little movement and only polite clapping came from the audience as the bland-sounding band seemed to be playing the same simple song over and over with just a slight change of words. Fortunately, Outrageously Normal proved to be a different story. Not corny or sappy, their love songs contained graceful intricate melodies that honestly reflected passion and desire. In one song, Dominick, the lead singer and guitarist, sang emotionally about the trials and angst of growing up.

"I wish we could see better," said Jayson. "I've heard he's supposed to be in his late thirties, maybe forty, but he looks much younger from back here."

"I heard he's incredibly handsome, but all I see is his stoppin' wavy brown hair," said Carmela.

"Why didn't I think to bring my mom's binoculars?" said Esmeralda.

"Yeah, why didn't you, Esmeralda?" said Garyd.

"Come on girl, let's dance!" said Bridget, and she and Carmela, while others were rocking their bodies around, broke into a confined-space waltz.

"I can't let you get away with that!" said Jayson, putting on a clumsy pirouette exhibition.

Esmeralda and Garyd snickered at their friends until their eyes met, then Garyd said, "Shall we dance, my love."

Quick as the beat he grabbed her hands and led her around in some type of modified tango, occasionally bumping into a forgiving soul.

"What are ya, a bunch of fairy queers?" blared from a set of powerful lungs.

The five looked. Behind them stood a group of men with capped heads, but also people with heads framed by long scraggly hair, and many other types of heads. It was unclear from which of the many accompanying mouths that comment had come.

"Loosen up buddy, they're only expressing themselves," said a young man with long red hair, who Esmeralda had spotted before. He returned to rolling his head in limber circles with eyes closed.

Esmeralda used this opportunity to really focus on the lyrics, staring at the stage in hopes of avoiding dancing with Garyd again. Outrageously Normal had moved on to a fiercer, more political song, a haunting anthem from years back, which was called "Thorns". Rolling and squeezing syllables in wherever he wanted without loosing clarity, melody or style, as was his gift and musical signature, and now more forceful with a coarse sandpaper throat, Dominick sang:

Roll out hatred's boxcars; they will take you no where.
Would you step off some clear day, so you could soar somewhere?
Will you wait until your deathbed to breathe the fresh unfurling air?
Ride in Satan's subway if you've got no view to spare.

We're the burrowed burr in that Mussolini suit.
Yes, we're the steely thorn inside the new Hitler's boot.

A few loud bellows for hatred drown out,
Brave sincere cries for a meaningful peace.
Useless information remembered and altered.
How many recall one truth time tries to teach?

Planet Variety keeps a comely house, a town named Contrast lies past Beaut.
And we're the steely thorn inside the new Hitler's boot.

When will the Nazis of this day wake up and realize,
Appearance, when it comes to treatment, should not matter? What's the matter?
If it did we would've hidden all of them by now,
Caged with some likeness of Manson's Mad Hatter.

Let's parade around in silver wear and proceed in peasant jute.
We'll never harm, but just stand up; words of reason will leave them mute.
They're eager for their power, but we'll never salute.
'Cause we're the steely thorn inside the new Hitler's boot.

So chilling was the melody that afterwards bodies seemed to twitch in one mass shiver. Listeners had left their doorways open, but now bolted them shut, at least momentarily.

The show finished off with several more love songs, then the entire congregation slipped away quietly, solemnly, their heads full of words, sounds, smells and (especially for those who arrived early enough) sights.

In the months following the concert, time passed quickly for Esmeralda. She had not said much to anyone about the details of that evening, for it all seemed rather superficial when she thought about it. Still, a bit of a new sense of life harboured within her, life from experiencing the freedom to be joyful. Her friends commented, one day asking her where her energy increase came from. "Same place as yours," was all she responded, then went back to wiping a table.

"Oh, I've seen how you love picking up the treasures people leave behind for you," teased Bridget.

"Sometimes working in a restaurant is like playing a game. Remember the right table. Find the gold, well, usually silver," said Esmeralda. She laughed. "In a zoo like this the challenge of the game is more rewarding than the tips." A distant look appeared on her face as she said to herself, "I prefer my treasures in winter gardens—rubies, turquoise, emeralds, with snowflakes of diamonds."

Bridget twisted her bejeweled nose. "What? Is that big bun putting too much pressure on your cranium?"

"Oh, I guess this hectic pace has me dreaming of another place," was Esmeralda's response.

Occasionally, Savannah returned to the smile-provoking thoughts inside Esmeralda's head. And, preciously, Christmastime came again. One busy night she came home from waitressing at around 11 o'clock and found that her parents were already in bed asleep. In the silence of the living room stood a completely decorated artificial cedar tree. A slight sadness came to her, for she had not had time to help with the decorating, and even now she needed to pass up the chance to look at the tree in favour of finding desperately needed sleep.

But as she started to walk past, she suddenly felt a strange pull toward the tree. She saw the trains and the aviary of birds and then she was hit by a strong smell coming from about twenty or thirty little green trees on strings, which it turned out were car air fresheners. She now regretted an earlier suggestion of hers that they have an artificial tree, but she honestly did not know that along with it came an artificial smell. *Must have been overstocked at the hardware store*, she figured. Then a more pleasing distraction took place. Noticing the crystal ornament with the lightning bolts, almost at eye level, yet remembering she had said she would not look into it again, she could not stop herself. Soon she was standing in a trance, just like Savannah.

This time the music came to Esmeralda sounding modern, yet psychedelic. She could picture the concert clearly. She saw herself finding the oak tree brooch, and wondering. Now she was standing at the concert with her friends, saying, "Why didn't I think to bring my mother's binoculars?" Next thing, flying over the stage was—how could this happen—the winged tiger?

"Not that philosophical feline again!" she cried.

The tiger seemed to pick out her cry. He bent his neck down to look at her. As he did, the camera bag slipped over his head and fell straight toward Esmeralda. She caught it with ease, and then proceeded to get out the camera, which still had the zoom lens attached.

Esmeralda heard the tiger growl out, "Well, how in the jungle am I supposed to land here with all these people?" And he flew on.

Looking through the camera's viewfinder, Esmeralda focused on the dark-haired Dominick—still distant. She zoomed in, but discovered that as she turned the camera lens, she herself actually moved closer. She also discovered that as she got closer, his hair changed. It was getting lighter. She was now close enough to see that indeed, he was surprisingly young looking and handsome and his hair was almost blonde.

In desperation, she yelled, "STOP!", and held the lens still, but it was too late; Dominick's slightly wavy, fairly shaggy, shoulder-tipping hair had crossed the border from mousy to golden. She could not turn it back. The lens would not zoom her away. She looked carefully at his broad, sturdy but not overbuilt shoulders and his rugged but sensitive face—a face that contradicted itself as its big gentle brown eyes were framed by thick dark sinister eyebrows that angled heavily toward a perfectly sculpted but imperfectly long Plasticine nose.

She watched his lips as they carefully molded each word he sang. He showed only an occasional smile, straight white top teeth dominating his whole face, including his crooked bottom teeth. Most of the time an expression of innocent joyful anguish filled his features and enveloped his voice—a voice that poured from his throat as smoothly as fine rich cream from a freshly glazed pitcher. He seemed so outlandish, almost like a sexy man from another galaxy, maybe even the next stage of human evolution. Yet, at the same time, he looked somewhat familiar. She tried to think who he reminded her of. *Yes, a bit like my old teacher Mr. Lobe, a bit like Nils Andreason, not at all like Garyd.* She stared, unblinking, at this cosmic creature for a period lasting what seemed a second and forever.

Suddenly something wavered through the air and onto the stage. Turquoise-encrusted, silver, triangular, it appeared to be enticing some of the band members. Dominick stopped playing and yelled, “Whatever you do, don’t touch that triangle! Believe me friends, I know what can happen and it’s not as wonderful as you might think.” Still, he had to hold the keyboard player back as the man tried to jump for it. The turquoise triangle floated away.

Dominick began to play his acoustic guitar in a flamenco style, then slowed in an adagio. He stared out into the crowd, moving his focus from side to side. When his eyes met Esmeralda’s, he quickly looked away and put down his guitar. The band moved into three-four time. Dominick climbed off the stage and walked over to her. She stood in shock as he pinned a glittering brooch to her tee-shirt, took her hand, put a gentle arm across her back, and began to whirl her in a light-footed waltz. The audience politely backed away to give them room. Then, she heard a young woman’s voice—she realized it was her own voice—singing, almost gasping, in a dry-throated whisper:

Mister Hair-Approaching-White,
You moved so whimsically tonight,
As you shimmied along the stage.
You should be covered in sweat,
But you’re not even wet;
Suspiciously younger than your age.

You leered through the crowd;
Placed your strings down.
How did those sailing eyes meet mine?
So, here I am in your arms,
I'll resist your snake charms,
But first I'll let you dance to the sky.

Oh, if my fantasies came true,
Angelcake, what would I do?
Would I be just as calm as I dream?
If swollen feet meet shrunken shoes,
Do both heels come unglued?
For mirages only trip a fantastic beam.

As you twirl me around
You swirl the sound,
As the band conjures up my direction.
Colours whirl me to a scene,
A causeway table—I am keen
To show worthiness of your attention.
So, you're impressed by my wit?
Well, I haven't spoken yet.
Just wait 'til you hear my soliloquy.
Now a waiter brings wine,
I don't need it—know my lines,
And you smile sugarcat—perceptively.

Oh, if I really met you,
White Warlock, what would I do?
Would I be the composition I dream?
Or would the trance be too much?
Would my brain need a crutch?
For visions reap longings—a book of reams.

Your ivy comes and begins
To cast its way through my skin;
Creeps through my insides vein by vein.

Vessels find uncharted parts.
Your vines pass right through my heart—
Use it—reach my struggling brain.
A leaf inside my palm
Pulls me out of my qualm
And leads me where dancing arms await.
Now my blood burns gold.
Dredge and savour my soul.
A simple waltz holds my hidden fate.

Oh, if I spun a spell on you,
Half-seraph, what would I do?
Become disappointed with my win?
You entice, that I know.
But that's part of the show.
I wonder who really lies within.

Is it better to live plain—
Engage the dull and mundane,
And let fantasies give us our light?
Or should we struggle for it all,
Face the risk of a fall,
To see if spotlights burn high and bright?

Yet to decipher my mind,
I'm looking at it one-eye-blind,
And patience for fame's a concern.
But, better a dreamer than not,
When dreams hold enchantment long sought.
New thoughts wisely taught me to learn.

Esmeralda continued to whirl and twirl and wistfully sing. As she did, she decided that she had better write this down somewhere because it so contradicted her old way of looking at the world and it was wonderful, yet so flaky, so much fun, but somewhat disturbing and not at all realistic. She would never fall for such a character in real life.

"If it isn't the waltzing waitress!" her pajama-clad mother could not help but let out a laugh as she entered the room.

"Care to dance Meteor Woman?" Esmeralda grabbed Maxine and gracefully guided her around the room. "I want to write a story—it just came to me."

"Will you send it to Savannah?"

"I guess I should, even though I won't hear back. Maybe I'll make a copy for her. I wonder if she still lives in Arizona? Maybe we should take a trip there sometime. I kind of wonder what it's like in other places, Mom. We don't travel much, do we? Except for Dad's visits to his first Town Plier."

"No, we don't and we should. There are so many spectacular places to see. The last few years life has been way, definitely, way too busy," Maxine paused. "Okay, but give us some time to figure out when it would work."

"Sounds yah-ma, Mama! And by the way, Mom, you smell wonderful—a lot better than the disgusting way you reeked when you smoked."

"Thanks, I suppose."

CHAPTER FOURTEEN

DANDELIONS AND WINTERGREEN

After sending her letter to Savannah, Esmeralda continued to come up with interesting bits to scratch onto paper, now even without the help of the carol sphere, for it appeared that the love of storytelling had come back to her in a new way. In a small notebook which she used as a journal she one day wrote:

The more I write, the more I wonder about and the stronger my desire to continue. How could I have been around for over eighteen years and for all that I know, hardly know a thing. Or so it seems. It's as though my knowledge is less than it once was, but I kind of like it, because I realize this doesn't mean I'm more ignorant... Now I will close my eyes and think up a new story...

With so much to contemplate as she finished her first year of photography classes, Esmeralda decided to take some time off from school to work, save up money and continue to wonder. While looking for work that had anything to do with a camera, she continued to waitress, now fulltime. Occasionally helping out at the Town Plier, hanging out with the Planarias—to her dismay, one day she realized that she too must be an inhabitant of Microscopia, for she fit right in with the group—dropping in for an occasional yoga rejuvenation, and riding her bike most places she went (she was now the only Planaria without a car) filled what was left of her time.

One drizzling day, just after she turned nineteen, Esmeralda sat down at a table with Carmela and Garyd after finishing her shift at the Funky Quarter. Gloree,

Garyd's ever-changing twin sister, was still working fulltime as a waitress, hobbling and wheeling her way, like a trained ape, through the meandering swarm of locusts, also known as "caffeinated customers," her head full of orders and momentarily memorized faces. Jayson, looking worried, stood over Mr. Wintergreen who was flopped over lifeless in his corner.

"Yeah, he's breathing!" he called out. "Guess he must really be out of it."

Mr. Wintergreen mumbled in his sleep. "Would birds be so wonderful if they were all seagulls? Ravens? Eagles? Peacocks...?"

The Planarias giggled at Jayson's confused expression.

"Don't interrupt me when I'm dreaming!" whispered Mr. Wintergreen. "Robins? Squirrels? Bears?"

"Hey, leave him alone," Zigzag said in a loud whisper. "He's been working two jobs. He's wiped. Don't you people know anything?"

"Sorry," whispered Jayson. "Just concerned, that's all." He joined his friends.

"So you two, how's university life?" asked Garyd.

"Do you want to hear the okay or the horrid?" Jayson replied.

"If you get what you want, the classes that is, it's not so bad," said Carmela. "I ended up with some moderately challenging and far from bland classes. Oh by the way, Esmeralda, I see your mom up there often. Isn't she about through the scholastic sandtrap?"

"Mom? Through the sandtrap? She's been using the wrong club. Actually I've lost track, but I think she's on the green, although lately she's been acting like she's my age or younger. She's been so chummy—she even wants to borrow my clothes. I wouldn't mind except she forgets to return them. Maybe once she starts working, at something other than the hardware store that is, she'll settle down a bit. Part of her slow progress comes because she takes all sorts of classes that aren't required, as though she's delaying graduation gratification.

"And, since this seems to be my pitching hour, I'll pitch all this off the forefront of my mind; the other thing that's annoying is that, suddenly, she bursts out singing on any slight cue. Is this what happens after they get over their mid-life crisis or just a part of it?"

"She's probably glad her cords are recovering after all that smoking, don't you think?" asked Jayson.

"Seriously, I think she's just happy, proud of herself 'cause she's doing what she wants to do."

"Is she an okay singer?" asked Garyd.

"Oh, she's pretty good. It's just that she's my mom so it sounds a little creepy coming from someone I know so well."

"I think I get it," said Carmela. "Kind of like when my parents do anything."

"Speaking of my mom, I told her I'd be home at 6:30, so I'd better flee like a freebie."

"Practice your asanas! You need 'em most when you're busy," said Carmela.

As Esmeralda picked up her umbrella and stood up she dropped an unclosed backpack from her lap. Books and papers slid out and spread to the next table.

"Never fear. I, Garyd, shall help you with that!" He bent over and helped pick up a few books, then came across a piece of paper which had fallen out of her journal. He looked at it for a minute, then said, "Holy! Every year they give out stupider literature to study no matter where you go to school."

"I'm not going to school right now, Garyd," Esmeralda reminded him.

"Listen to this." He laughed and put on his most knightly intonation. " 'In Salingmar of old, yes, so you're now told, stood the land of Enrapture, kept out of reach of the Encroachers of Encapture—' "

Esmeralda heard the others giggling. She jerked the

story out of Garyd's hands and with nostrils flared said, "Thanks a lot for laughing, guys! Garyd, you really rub my wings the wrong direction." As she stormed out into the rain, Carmela chased after her.

"I can't believe I actually shared Mom's womb with you, Garyd!" yelled Gloree, gathering dishes from an empty table.

Jayson called, "Glow to the sky Esmeralda, like you do. We love you!"

"Let me walk you to the bus," said Carmela. "I'm really sorry for laughing. We didn't know you'd written that. We weren't laughing at the writing anyway, just the way Garyd was acting. You know, Garyd is actually Quasimodo about you. I bet he's feeling like a nimrod now. He just acts like a fool to get attention; neither he or Gloree ever got any at home, their parents are hardly ever there. You know that. Actually, it's surprising neither kid has gotten into any serious trouble." She smiled. "He's especially foolish when he's around you. Don't tell me you didn't notice."

"I didn't," said Esmeralda, trying to hold back a sob and force her umbrella open at the same time. "Besides, Garyd's the last organism I would be interested in."

"Zerve, Esmeralda, you know Garyd isn't really such a drudge. He won't be packing groceries forever—"

"This is not an occupation issue, Carmela! I have no problem with grocery types."

"Well, he's nice too, even though I know he doesn't show it often. A long time ago, when Jayson's family just moved to Canada, Garyd was the only one who was friendly toward him. People followed him after awhile and started treating Jayson better, but at first some people were really cruel—hit him over the head with books, stuff like that. Even though he sometimes gets frustrated with Garyd, Jayson's actually grateful to him."

"So, that's it. That's why he puts up with him!"

The bus pulled up to the curb.

Before the soaked Carmela dashed off, she turned and implored, "Think about Garyd Nichols, okay Esmeralda?"

If that was not enough for one day, as Esmeralda watched people get off the bus, she was taken by surprise by one of the departees who stared at her as he put up his umbrella. It was the blonde and dashing Dominick. A young scarf-headed man, who was working on becoming a drenched-headed man, accompanied him. He carried a guitar case.

"Esmeralda, are you going? Don't tell me we just missed you again!" said Dominick.

"We'll have to get our timing right one of these days," said the scarf-headed guy.

"G-g-gotta go!" stuttered Esmeralda. As she climbed onto the bus she instinctively handed her umbrella to the drenched one.

In response, he reached into his coat pocket. He handed her a piece of plastic, chocolate-brown.

Garyd? Esmeralda had no interest in thinking about Garyd on the way home. As the rain turned to sleet, her mind, every brain cell it seemed, was occupied by and with this Dominick character. *A hallucination*, she thought, *for he is not a real person, not the blonde Dominick, that is. Such a quick glimpse that I had. Probably someone with a slight resemblance. But why would he look for me, whoever he was? And who was that scarved creature? A band member? Sort of a caddie—carrying Dominick's guitar? Not likely.* She examined the piece of brown plastic, somewhat triangular but rounded. *A guitar pick*, she realized. After supper she would have to seek the answers.

"Could you use a hand with anything, Mom? Dad?"

"No," answered Maxine. "You just relax. You look tired."

"Can you believe Christmas is coming already? It'll be here before we know it!" said Esmeralda.

"I guess we have some gettin' ready to do, eh?" said Bill.

"Need any help?"

"I thought we told you to relax, Gem," said Maxine.

"It's just this house doesn't seem Christmassy."

"Okay. You're right. Let's haul out some boxes and see what we find," said Bill.

A fresh energy lifted Bill and Esmeralda out of their chairs. In a short time they had found and sorted through two boxes. Esmeralda sat on the floor, crouching over something she held in her hands.

Maxine yelled from the kitchen, "Go have a bath, kiddo, it'll help you feel better."

Esmeralda decided that her mother did have the occasional good idea, after all. She took the carol sphere with her, handling it carefully as she set up the bath. Immersed in warm water, except for her face and the hand that held the sphere, she quietly inquired, "Only you can tell me why I saw Dominick today. Is it true that I've been working too hard, trying to do too much? Has Garyd finally driven me over the edge? Are there such things as ghosts? Please tell me I'm not losing my mind."

Water waved back and forth around her ears, its sound preventing Esmeralda from making out the sound of the carol. Presently, the sphere was filled with Dominick's face, hauntingly distorted by the curvature of the ornament. She let her whole head go underwater. When her eyes emerged they examined a different face—Mr. Wintergreen's. He spoke directly to her, the craggy lines around his eyes, forehead and mouth exaggerating his expressions:

"It all depends on how you say something. Anything

sounds idiotic if it is mimicked. Your story means something to me, so I should tell it. Now you listen to this calm, wise and respectful modulation." She was first entertained by floating images, vivid, yet as if from another person's fantasy. It started with dandelions, but the detail grew—by the small, swift strokes of an artist's brush:

In Salingmar of old, yes, so you're now told, stood the land of Enrapture, kept out of reach of the Encroachers of Encapture. Their gate was a string of lions and dragons and knights who were actually harmless but appeared formidable, and thus kept others away.

While the fine lions trounced the abundant dandelions of the border, the knights and dragons picked the flowers for their game of dandelion pinochle. All of the Queens of Spades and Hearts were in the audience, but were continuously glancing at their children, fours and fives, who were wandering as they played leapfrog charades in the thickets by a brook. The Spade children were prettier, but the Heart children more agile, and so it was, and the queens fought no more as they had done in the past.

When the game was over and the scoretrees set back to zero, the Queens of Spades left and all the Queens of Hearts became empty inside and plain, for their vibrant red hearts went with their friends. The Queens of Hearts were now entrusted with all the children, Heart and Spade, who were bobbing for the amazing sinking balloons in the effervescent potholes of the brook.

No one ever knew what happened in or to the Land of Enrapture until now. You are listening to a voice released from the past because my grain of sand has at last been excavated.

Ancient cultures roar as they speak.
They roar as they speak—they've been buried so deep.
To learn of them all's

Beyond a lifetime's recall.
So learn of the ones that will come,
listen again.
And keep turning the hourglass until the end.

And one Queen of Hearts took off her hat and let her long hair follow as the Queens of Spades descended under the Bridge of the Forever Falling Leaves. They stopped to unbury a helpless mouse, then continued on, guiding the wind, guiding the hair.

The dust and the mortar,
the sandmaker's query.
We will eat lemondrops
and drink from the berry.
While we piece together ruins,
gluing grains one by one,
we ask a simple question—
"Is anything ever done?"

Is there a moral to this story? No. Unless you see one in it. Just feel honoured that someone told you. You are among the few who know. Although the stories held within us are the ones that most matter. We will learn from the past while we learn as we go (and now we know how we sow what we grow). And the longhaired empty-hearted queen said:

"Love yourself, then forget yourself,
then love yourself again.
The hours keep on turning, churning—
an old forgotten friend.
Love yourself, then forget yourself,
think of a long-lost friend.
Our thoughts will keep on burning, yearning,
until they meet again."

She looked at the children who were picking cherries for the dragons and wondered if life could get better and she knew what she had to do:

Whisper, love me now.
  I can't.
Love me now.
  I can't.
I have to love others instead.

A Queen of Spades' words echoed from a distant fjord:

Release the pieces; shuffle the deck;
Flip the cards; double knight check.
No hand of love 'til to others you've dealt.
Then deal yourself and watch their dice melt.
'You may hold hands,' the game has said.
Light-stepping to the next square, all move ahead.

And all the Hearts beamed. They knew that many squares were still to come. Some quick hops, some not. They turned around together and there appeared a castle of one hundred doors, one hundred turrets and one hundred spires floating on a sea of wind-feathered snow.

And the truest peace stayed with Enrapture for many years. Eventually, though, someone forgot what they held. Now I must join the other cognizant grains from past civilizations so that we can come together and build a shrine which will be an oasis. And people can choose a time and land from our collage or, better, mandela, and we will tell them a story:

Can you hear us calling?
Where do we come from?
Does it matter?
What do you think?

Esmeralda spoke through the vision. "I'll be. Am I that forward?"

"Are you?" Mr. Wintergreen's deep, resonant presentation became like a song as he swayed with hunched shoulders and skimmed the horizon with his dark wrinkled fingers. His round eyes stared straight at Esmeralda:

In case you are wondering who,
Is this old mechanic who's tellin' you.
They call me Sandcastle Wintergreen,
Blackest Santa you've ever seen.

He continued to speak, but Esmeralda caught sight of her own wrinkled fingers and subsequently pushed herself up and out of the tub. Her dripping hands almost dropped the sphere, but she gained control in time and carefully placed it on the counter. Later, she hung it on their Christmas tree.

Esmeralda made herself a pouch. Her sewing skills were not the best, and the pouch did not look like it had been made in India—it was actually made from the blue denim she had cut off her jeans while making shorts. It served its purpose, however. She needed a place to put all of the strange little items that she had received. Into the pouch went the oak tree brooch and the guitar pick, the letter from Savvy and her address, a photo she had taken of the carol sphere, and a ticket stub from the Outrageously Normal concert. She spotted her journal and figured, since it was a record of "strange little events," it too should be housed in the pouch. Last, she rolled up the story she had written, like a scroll, tied a ribbon around it and placed it inside.

CHAPTER FIFTEEN

ARIZONA CALLS

February at the Funky Quarter.

"...really sounds like a Generation X 'tude you're loadin', Garyd," said Jayson.

"Hey, Jay, I know I'm under their influence—a lot of them in our neighbourhood."

Carmela glowered. "The Apathetics, you mean?" She smiled impishly. "Some call us 'Ys', you know. Among other things."

"How does it feel to be a 'Y'?" Esmeralda said, eyes rolling.

Jayson held his hands to his heart, "Y oh Y oh Y."

"Y do they have to go and label us?" asked Carmela.

"Y couldn't they come up with a more exciting label for us. Say, 'Generation Asteroid'," said Garyd.

"'Generation Comet' would sound even faster," Jayson said.

"Instead of being the 'Lost Generation', can we be the 'Found Generation'?" asked Esmeralda.

"Where do you suppose they'll find us?" asked Jayson. "Y not no title. I guess then they'd start calling us the 'Untitled Generation'."

Carmela choked out, "We would be 'The Generation Formerly Known as Y'. No name, just a symbol."

"There must be people whose jobs are to just come up with labels for people," Garyd added.

"It's like this bumper sticker I saw the other day: 'Confuse the Demographers—Be Yourself'," Carmela said.

"I hate to sound stupid," said Garyd, "but since that's the general consensus anyway, I'll go ahead and ask: What are demographers?"

Jayson answered, "You're not stupid, Garyd. You

just have some things to learn. Like all of us. Demographers are people who categorize other people based on which body parts they can be seen scratching in public."

"Hilarious, Jay. Real hilarious. Ugh!" Carmela said. "But I'm sure Garyd gets the idea. Anyhow, they shouldn't compare us to previous generations. Each one of us will have our own opinion, our own way."

"Then that settles it. We'll be 'Generation Undefinable, Indescribable, Individual'," Esmeralda stated.

"Guess what Esmeralda?" said Carmela. "Gloree Nichols and I have saved up enough. Remember that trip to India we talked about? We're going to do it. August. Can we talk you into it?"

"No. Can't afford it. Besides, for some reason India doesn't seem to be calling me these days. I hope it will one day—"

"Hey, wait a minute," interrupted Jayson. "How can you afford to go Carmela? Seeing that you have all those university expenses."

"Well, um, Jayson, my parents have helped me with my university."

"Oh yeah? Hmm, tell me how much, Poor Girl."

"Do I really have to?"

" 'Fraid so!"

"All of it," Carmela said, hiding her face.

"And all this time you've been bugging me about being rich? You devil."

"I'll buy you lunch, Jayson."

"No food handouts, please. But buy me a trip to India, then I'll forgive you. Just kidding, Poor Girl!"

"Is that where you'd choose to go, Jayson?" asked Esmeralda.

"Do they like Chinese people in India?" asked Jayson.

"Don't know. Probably," said Carmela. "Where would you go, Esmeralda?"

"My mom said something about us going to Arizona a while back. She probably forgot. You remember how I talked about my friend Savvy. I wish I could see her again. I wish I could explain why. I can't describe her. Amazing's the best word." Esmeralda concentrated for a moment. "I remember one time when I was at a fair with Savvy and a woman we didn't know came up to us and I thought we were going to get lip for something, but she said, 'Your friend must be the most spontaneously happy person I have ever seen. She just radiates harmony.' I wondered why I didn't feel jealous of Savvy, but eventually decided that it was just because it was somehow meant to be that way."

Back at home, Esmeralda carefully approached Maxine. "Mom? Do you remember how we talked about visiting Arizona sometime?"

"Yes. And you're probably wondering what this lady has done about it and your hunch is right—nothing. Sorry. I wonder what it would be like there. Your father and I were there so many sunsets ago, back when we were first together, but I can't remember it too well. I guess my focus was on him."

"Tell you what, I'll let you in on a secret—a mysterious, dark, enticing, juicy, musical, sensational, incandescent, optical, prismatic, chromatic secret." Esmeralda recited her teaser in a most scintillating manner.

"Sounds the best. Roll 'em Camera Lady."

"Observe, Meteor Woman." Esmeralda took Maxine to the closet. "Ever have Christmas in February?" She quickly found the carol sphere.

"Is this where we imitate Savannah?" asked Maxine.

"You could say that. Now stare in here. Deeply. You usually don't get the vision you want, I'll warn you, but try."

Maxine and Esmeralda stood still and stared as together they held the ornament's embroidery thread loop.

Maxine said softly, "Do you remember the 'Winter Carol' I used to sing to you as we decorated the tree when you were little? I can sing it again." And softly she sang the song that Esmeralda had heard so many times within the sphere.

When the carol and its accompanying magazine-collage parade were over and only a vision of a candle remained, Esmeralda looked even further into the depths of the warming sphere and then she was there, under the blazing Arizona sun. Surrounded by a ramshackle ghost town, she found herself dressed in a short white dress with blue polka dots and short puffy sleeves. Barefoot and with arms behind her back, she walked, then leisurely skipped and twisted down the dusty road that separated the rumpled shacks into two opposing outlaw gangs. As the sand squirted in puffs between her wide-stretched toes, she heard a bluesy guitar play a slowly sliding accompaniment to her lilting movements.

She zigzagged back and forth across the road, peering into each window and imagining what may have taken place in another time. Alone, she let her hair out of its bobby pin prison. Her head fell back as she spread her arms to accept the heat on its own terms. As she lifted her head, she thought she saw someone out of the corner of her eye. She believed she had seen a guitar player on one of the roofs. A blonde one. But when she looked again, there was no one in sight. Time to move on.

Soon Esmeralda materialized in the middle of a desert, surrounded by brilliant flowering cactus and other succulents, only one of which she could identify—the prickly pear cactus, her nemesis. It reminded her of Julieanne. Not because of its prickly nature and not because Julieanne was a nemesis, although seeing similarities in the two could not be avoided. Rather, it had to do with the fact that Julieanne had once loaned her mother a book entitled *Des Chisholm's Album of*

Salad Succulents. That had led her mother to plant at least twenty of the dangerous monsters all around the outside of their house, forcing an annoyed Esmeralda to wear shoes whenever she stepped out. She could still recall her "innocent" explanation to her mother upon the prickly pears' death, "I just thought that if they had lots of water throughout each day, they'd have stored up enough to survive a dry summer."

These Arizona prickly pears, however, were strong and healthy with needles that said "vengeance," and Esmeralda carefully gauged each step of her tender feet.

It seemed to her that she was lost, for she had no idea which way to go or where she had come from. *That's what happens when one materializes in the middle of the desert.* Most bothersome, though, was the fact that her nose was so dry that it itched inside and out and she could not tell whether anything smelled. Boredom was coming fast, but not as fast as worry.

Then, as if torn from the pages of a fairy tale, a horseback rider appeared in the distance and galloped toward her, looking like he was on a mission. Esmeralda, to her relief, could make out a dark-haired man on a sturdy brown mustang. A few seconds later, now much closer, she saw that his hair was much lighter and that it was continuing to lighten.

"Oh, no! Stop! I mean, WHOA!" shouted Esmeralda.

"Whoa!" yelled the rider as he pulled back on the reins. It was too late, though. He was the blonde Dominick again, complete with guitar strapped to his back.

"Have you come to haunt me or taunt me, man of the vision that won't come true!" screamed an infuriated Esmeralda.

"I am searching. From a distance I caught sight of you and I thought you might be able to help me solve this trying conundrum I've been living with for the past eleven years. I thought maybe you knew enough about the native plants, seeing that you are out here in the middle of this desert garden."

"Wrong person. Now leave me alone. But first, what is with your shirt?" Esmeralda had observed that his shirt kept changing colour as he moved.

"Oh yes, my shirt. Do you see the solar panels down the sleeves? That's where the power comes from. The micro-lenses pick up the hues and brilliance of my surroundings; the computer chip in the cuff link then calculates the exact colour my shirt should be to contrast those surroundings, to make me stand out. It's a special fabric—has something to do with fiber optics woven into each thread. Reserve power is stored in this solar-saver pack in my chest pocket. Shirt's really for performing, but I thought I'd test it while I was out here on my quest."

"Somehow I'm not surprised I gave you a power pack!" Esmeralda moaned.

"You didn't give this to me." He wrinkled his nose in a way that only looked cute on him. "What are you talking—"

"Oh, my mistake. I didn't." She let a short burst of air blast from her nose. "I can't believe this!"

"You're not lost are you?" asked Dominick.

She despised the sympathetic smile he wore, but said, "I suppose I have to 'fes up to it."

"Well, I'm just going to look a little bit more, then I can give you a ride home."

Esmeralda looked straight at this contrary-coloured chameleon. "You don't know how far away I live."

"Of course I do, Esmeralda. Now, you can help me. Here are the clues. Tell me if you see any of these items:

Rub quickly for about an hour:
A root given to you by another,
Fuzz of tiger's wing,

A water-ringed dry thing,
And the most phenomenal flower,
All wrapped in blue servant of the shower."

"Isn't that funny you thought of Arizona as where to look?" laughed Esmeralda.

"It seemed logical to me," said Dominick. "I figured the winged tiger might like the warmth here. And there are some pretty phenomenal flowers. But you disagree?"

"Yes, but, well, I might be able to help you," she droned without conviction. "But, first, tell me, this has suddenly gotten me nosy and I wish I weren't, I shouldn't care, but why do you need these things? What is this riddle all about?"

"That was the inscription on the turquoise triangle—the English inscription that is. It was fine print, hard to read, so I just hope I got it right."

"You mean you touched the turquoise triangle?" She paused, then said, "I almost did, too, but nearly fell off the...well, the tiger."

"Yeah, the triangle is often near the tiger. The tiger flies over our performances every so often. Likes our rhythms. So one day I saw this triangle, it was while we were warming up, actually, and I had no idea what it was, but it was annoying me because it kept dipping down in front of my face, so I grabbed it. I wanted to throw it like a Frisbee, but I couldn't let go of it. I felt an intense vibration—like all my ions were being exchanged, that's the only way I can think of to describe it. Then I read it—the antidote. A minute later, the triangle just floated out of my hand. Oh, but be glad you didn't touch it, Gem."

"Why?"

"I have learned that what happens is it reverses aging. For the past eleven years I've been getting younger instead of older. I get to keep my memories, and those aid in developing wisdom, but otherwise I'm in retrograde motion."

"I thought you looked younger than when I danced with you, but not quite as handsome, I am happy to say. Your face is lacking shape. What's wrong with getting younger, though? Isn't that what your generation aims for? Or don't you like young people?"

"At first I thought it wonderful, exciting, refreshing. It has definitely given me ideas for my songs. Opened my mind to new ways of looking at the world. I can't deny that having all this energy is a thrill. But, while all that seems fine, being young isn't always easy. You must know that."

"I know this part ain't easy!"

"Why don't you climb on and I'll take you home now."

Esmeralda decided she'd be fine riding double with this man, since it was, after all, only a fantasy. And his guitar was still on his back, so she could lean against it instead of him. Onto the horse, now a palomino, she climbed.

Dominick continued, "Seems the younger you look the less credibility you have. I long for the days when people would take me seriously—listen to my opinion. I must seem self-conscious, but how can you believe in yourself when nobody takes you seriously? You can only do it by continuously reassuring yourself. Seems self-centered. That bothers me. Or else completely ignore others reactions if that's possible. It would be easy to stop trying to express myself if I didn't know better. I still call a lot of the shots, but I let the other band members talk to the public now. That way the message gets across. I find that I now rely so much on intuition. My thoughts come so fast, but it's so hard to articulate them because they don't always come in words, but often in images or gut feelings."

Esmeralda enjoyed seeing Dominick get riled, yet she sympathized. "Go on."

"Because I can't put a statement together easily and

I jumble what I'm saying, people believe I have nothing to say. They just look at this unweathered face and assume I haven't lived—that I'm shallow. They don't know I'm writing the best songs of my career."

"You make sense to me."

"That's because you're giving me a chance." He continued, "Then there are those who expect me to be more of a rebel. A troublemaker. Of course being a rock star, I can't go as far as to act pious, that would border on hypocrisy, but it's also hypocritical to sing of love and then run around acting like a complete buffoon. I'm only a partial one."

"Maybe you should be talking to Garyd."

"Okay, I'm mellowing. It has been an intriguing experience. You know, sometimes with age comes a jadedness, a closed mind. Energetic and fresh ideas should be listened to with wisdom, patience and openness."

She quipped, "Sometimes the young can be jaded. We have our own form."

"I'm glad you're the one who said it."

Esmeralda decided to add a suddenly found opinion, partly to see what his reaction would be. "I think older people are actually jealous of the young—the fact that we have all those years and adventures ahead of us, not behind."

"It's quite possible they're jealous of your beauty, too, forgetting that they had their time of beauty and still do..."

"Is he a charmer or what?" Esmeralda smirked.

"But from what I've experienced, many older people really do care. Even if it's hard for them to remember how they viewed this planet when they were young. Even if they have changed, perhaps we humans sense that each of us will change; we just weren't made to stay the same through our entire lives. We can't hold it against each other that we're all at different stages."

"So you would like to reverse it again and start getting old?"

Dominick twisted around, slid the guitar from his back to his front and let his long thin knobby-knuckled fingers strum a chocolate-brown pick through the strings. Esmeralda noticed how light his shirt was getting and how dark the sky had become.

"Am I ready? It won't be long until I am. I hope that I have what I need and it all works. I would truly prefer to finish life in a nursing home than as a starving street urchin."

"Is that what happens?"

"From what I gather it is. Now, I'm eager to find out how you can help me."

Esmeralda paused a moment, for, naturally, she was not going to be overly kind. "See this pouch I'm carrying? I'll give it to you when I get home. It should have all the items you need in it."

"Looks like it came from someplace in the Far East. It's gorgeous. It's fortunate you happen to have it with you."

"Yeah, India's where I got it. I think I take it with me on all my fantasies."

"What makes you think this is a fantasy?"

"Hey, Blondie, I know it is. What I can't figure out is why I saw you that day in reality—at the bus."

"I don't remember that. What makes you think that was reality?"

"I guess it was real, but it wasn't reality. Or maybe vice-versa."

Breathtaking rock formations shone against the darkening sky. A few minutes later, Dominick's shirt beamed a lactescent white. Esmeralda thought its brightness would prevent her from falling asleep, but eventually she ended up slumbering against Dominick's back with her arms around him as she drooled on his pretty shirt.

She awoke with a start. "Am I out of this mirage yet?"

The cause of her waking was Dominick, half-panicking, ripping off his optical display to reveal a white undershirt. Esmeralda thought the undershirt suited him better anyway.

"It must be spitting rain. My shirt's crackling. Doesn't get along with water." He threw the shirt on the ground, cursing. "Hellion of a superficial scavenger. Why do I get brainwashed into these promotional idiocies?" Shortly, he was laughing. "Why do you keep saying things like that, though? About mirages and fantasies."

He then settled down enough to return to strumming on his wooden love. "We crossed the border, the Peace Arch, just a few minutes ago. While you were asleep."

Esmeralda asked him to stop the horse so that she could get off.

"I'm sorry. Did I offend you?"

"No. It's because I now realize the time has come to do my run. You see, I am searching, too, but for what I don't know. Maybe for my friend. Maybe for an answer. Maybe for a cause. Oh look, surreal! See a banner way up ahead? That must be the finish line. Please, let me off."

Dominick stopped and she slid off. She discovered that she was carrying two pouches, the "fantasy" pouch from India, plus the "real" pouch she had made from blue denim. Temptation told her to give him the denim pouch, but she thought for a moment, then handed him the beautiful pouch from India. As she did, he bent over and kissed her hand. She could not stand the way it tingled so nicely.

At first Esmeralda could only hobble, but with each step her stride became longer and her feet became lighter until she was running effortlessly. As she approached the banner, jovial people lined the streets and cheered. Breaths of the purest air she had ever encountered kept her moving. She was now accompanied by thousands of runners joining the pack from many angles. Soon she could read the banner that stretched ten blocks long and several storeys high. "WE DID IT!" was printed in house-sized letters. She was ready to run under the banner, but was forced to stop just when she reached it. A mass of people stood blocking the way.

She looked straight at the person in front of her and felt surprised when she realized it was herself. Looking right into a mountain-sized mirror, one suitable for the most swollen head ever, she saw people of all ages and colours holding hands, laughing, crying joyfully, hugging, singing and generally carrying on. Beyond the crowd she surveyed the world as it should be—flowering hills, tall trees, a utopian blue sky and Dominick, his hair and horse darkening as he rode away. Suddenly his image enlarged. She could see him rummaging through the pouch; scrutinizing the bit of tiger's wing, the root, the dried jug and the blue towel; deeply smelling the purple and green striped flower; then turning his head and grinning like a child, his eyebrows never higher.

With a faraway look in her eyes, Esmeralda said to herself. "Is this something that will happen one day? Could any of this happen?" She started searching through the denim pouch.

Two harmonious voices piped in, each familiar and with a high and a low pitch, "This is what could happen. We are not predictors of the future. We are only predictors of possibilities. That did not rhyme."

"Wow, that was an amazing vision!" Maxine exclaimed.

"Did you see what you wanted?" asked Esmeralda.

"Yes, but more! The Grand Canyon visited in fine form! I saw it in so much detail. I examined each layer carefully. Don't remember noticing so much before—

the intensity of it. I never realized there were so many shades of amber!"

"Figures," sighed Esmeralda.

"Is life an unrealistic imitation of fantasy? Why do you look at me so? I'm not serious child. Just trying too hard to be humorous, I guess. Anyway, that vision makes the decision for me. How's that for sounding like an ad? Well, we're going to Arizona this summer, regardless. I'm writing to Julieanne right now, so go find me the address, Esmeralda Zoomer. And while you're at it, don't forget to check your film supply."

PART THREE

CHAPTER SIXTEEN

TRAVEL SLUGS

It was settled. The Mrkys would head to Arizona in early May, hoping to avoid the most vicious heat and not to avoid the Andreasons. They waited to see if Maxine's letter would summon a return of information.

Meanwhile, at the Funky Quarter, the steps of the staff were frothier than the cappuccino they served. Spring days, impending trips and rapid business were mainly responsible for the overly perky behaviour of the employees.

"Let's do something for Easter. I've got the travel bug. Who can go on a jaunt?" asked Carmela.

Everyone except Carmela had to work.

"Come on, Zigzag. Let Esmeralda Mrky have a break. She's been working too hard. She needs some adventure."

"Okay, those whose last name is Mrky gets four days off, but nobody else asks. You hear?"

"Hey, thanks Zigzag!" said Esmeralda.

"Yeah, thanks Zig. Where do you want to go? Besides Arizona—not enough time," said Carmela.

"You sure give a person a millennium to consider things," chided Esmeralda. "A place where I can really practice my photography is all I ask. Someplace scenic."

Carmela spoke slowly. "Wintergreen would suggest your homeland if he was here. Why don't you show me where you used to live? Cowichan Lake, wasn't it?"

"Yeah, haven't seen the old homestead for a few.

Taking your car, Carmela? Seeing I don't have one."

"Yup. We'll take a tent too. Sorry you can't come Harpreet Nichols, but remember India's next up."

Fiddling with her jet-black hair, Harpreet, who had now changed her name from Gloree, did not seem bothered. She had appeared to be in her own meditative world ever since plans had been made for the India trip.

Early on Good Friday morning, two young ladies plus one full-grown Desdemona Gravity Defier were up and out and on an early ferry to Nanaimo. Carmela's old grey Ford was stuffed with all kinds of backpacking gear and food and a survival kit for Carmela with her compass, herbal hair formulas and natural-look makeup. Esmeralda had sneaked the carol sphere into the car, wrapped in paper towels. She hoped that if she looked into it at the place where she used to really see Savannah, maybe the girl's face would come back to her. It was even harder now to picture her.

As she had promised her father, Esmeralda asked Carmela to stop at her Uncle Stan's house to say hello and meet his new wife Lannie. When they got out of the car, Desdemona found a large wooden wolf, a chainsaw carving of Stan's, to sniff at.

"Good place to tie you, eh?" said Carmela. "Right here attached to your new friend."

When the door opened, was Esmeralda ever in a state of dropping-jaw. She recognized Lannie as the same cashier she had seen in Chemainus who, when Savvy was upset, Julieanne showed her passport to. Lannie did not seem to remember her though.

Introductions. Weather talk. Ferry talk. Assorted niceties. Then Stan broke pattern, "See Lannie, I told you she was a little tiny sweetheart of a child."

Fine. Esmeralda could handle comments like that without getting annoyed, but unfortunately Lannie had come from a similar mold as her husband, only cast with ditches where Stan had divots.

"I remember now, Stan. She's the niece you said everybody worries 'bout 'cause she's such a frail little thing. Now be honest, are you two really going backpacking? Two women? Doesn't sound like my idea of pleasure—carrying some heavy bag all day through spiderwebs, slugs and bugs. Why don't you just stay here for the weekend? Rest your precious selves."

Esmeralda inquired, "Who is 'everybody,' Stan? Who worries about me?"

"Oh, not sure, probably just me. I'll mention though, Esmeralda, it looks like you've made it through teenagerhood dent-free. Only a chip on the shoulder."

"She looks upset, Stan," said Lannie. "Hmm, sensitive girl."

"Oh, she knows I'm joshin'. Seriously, you should rest here...some movies in the listings or we could rent an action flick."

Carmela came to her companion's rescue. "The woods is the best place to get the kind of rest we need. Nice and quiet. You wouldn't believe how noisy that restaurant gets."

"Oh, yes I can!" stated Lannie. "The gift shop in Chemainus gets just as noisy, I am sure! But I tolerate it well. We get strange customers—probably from Victoria. I should tell you about this one girl who came in who was so undisciplined...where was her mother's head? So this girl comes in and starts yelling for her mommy over and over, and—"

Esmeralda interrupted, knowing full well that she was taking a risk. "Sounds like the girl had autism."

"Do you really think so? How do you know? No, I'm positive she didn't. She could talk and everything. No, I've seen autistics before and she was not one. Just bad upbringing."

"What if I said I was there. I was. I know the girl."

"Oh, you're thinking of something else. You

would've been too young to remember." insisted Lannie.

Carmela chimed as though she belonged in a gift shop, "Nice meeting you, Stan Mrky and Lannie. Esmeralda has to go now 'cause she's got a pushy friend who doesn't think she should waste her time on people who don't consider the possibilities. Don't hold it against her."

Esmeralda added, "Don't hold it against Carmela. She's only pushy 'cause sometimes I need a push. Bye."

Together the two friends stumbled out the door, and found Desdemona dragging the wooden wolf behind her as she jogged in circles around the lawn, leaving several bare patches in the grass. While Carmela untied her dog, Esmeralda looked back at the porch and saw Stan and Lannie standing still with their arms folded while they shook their heads in disapproval.

"Sorry Stan," said Esmeralda.

"I won't make you pay," grumbled Stan as he turned to walk inside.

As they drove on, Esmeralda declared, "My parents mentioned Stan had changed, but I didn't believe them. I thought they didn't know that side of him before. But he's worse. Maybe, as they said, he really does need a midlife shake to loosen him."

"It'll take more than that for Lannie," murmured Carmela. "Anyhow, I'm looking forward to seeing your old place. Must be fabulous."

Esmeralda was saddened, however, when they reached Honeymoon Bay and saw her old home, for it was now dilapidated, likely abandoned. While Desdemona waited in the car, Esmeralda took Carmela over to the dome cabin. It was holding up better than her old house, but still looked like it needed a good staining. She decided to knock, but was not surprised when there came no answer.

With the carol sphere in her hand, she paused on the

front porch, carefully unwrapped the paper towels and fixed her eyes into the middle of the ornament. She saw something flitting—a willowy wisp that floated down the trail to the lake. She rewrapped the sphere and, in a nimble-footed fashion, ventured down to where the wisp had gone. She could almost hear voices from the past and splashing sounds. She walked to the end of the dock and carefully studied her reflection.

"What am I expecting to see here? I see myself. Funny, but I don't look ugly, and, yet I don't look like a swan either. I don't look somewhere in-between. I just look like me. That's all I see. I like that."

Carmela called to her from the edge of the woods, "All this water makes me feel like whizzing a leak. There wouldn't be a johnny pot nearby?"

"I have the same problem. Forest here we come!"

Behind an oak tree, Esmeralda started to pull down her pants, but heard a nearby sound—someone whistling a tune. "Carmela, don't go yet. Someone's near," she quietly called to her friend who was about to mark territory at the next tree over.

Carmela, zipper still down, scurried, not unlike a mischievous storybook squirrel, over to her friend. At the same time they both spotted the whistler. He had been walking the shoreline, but now was scanning the bush in their direction. He called out, "Anyone there?" then continued his stroll of the lake edge, now humming.

Esmeralda whispered, "Are you the saviour in disguise or the antichrist acting sacred, kind. I can't believe this, it's Dominick again. He looks even younger than I remember. I guess he hasn't reversed yet. What am I saying?"

"I have no idea. Dominick who? The singer? That's not him. But he is a babe. I've seen that face before. Somewhere. Wish I could remember where." Carmela stared until he was out of sight. "Ah! Honey Man Bay."

Several minutes later Carmela went back to her car and retrieved Desdemona. They took her for a short walk, then decided they'd better find a campsite. Into the car and off, Carmela drove while Esmeralda turned around to give the dog a good long pet.

"Hey, look! A Shervonian Shepherd!" expressed Carmela. "I didn't think you'd see one this far removed."

Esmeralda turned around. "A what? Wait, turn right, not left. We're heading for the campground, right? At Gordon Bay? Huh, what's that Desdemona? Yes, we'll be doing a brain scan on her real soon. Besides, you're in good hands when I'm along."

After turning, Carmela responded, "One day I'll tell Desdemona about some of the strange things you've done, Esmeralda. Good thing she didn't hear that bit about Dominick not reversing. I have a feeling this trip will do us some good."

CHAPTER SEVENTEEN

SISTERS OF THE MIST

Esmeralda had forgotten how delightful Gordon Bay could be in the off-season. After taking pictures of the place she and her uncle used to criticize, the two excited travellers settled into a campsite. After the wooden wolf episode they did not dare tie Desdemona to their tent. Instead they found a sturdy tree, tied her, put a blanket around her and took turns cuddling her to sleep. The two human members of the expedition knew they should also get to sleep early because they were heading for a big day of backpacking, but it was hard to stop talking. Something about wanting to sleep gives one so much to talk about.

"Whenever I visit such a beautiful place I get so inspired," said Carmela. "We have to do whatever we can to preserve. And to heal the damage."

"I agree, but it's an enormous responsibility to mend the world. Are we up to it? What do we do about travelling, for example?" asked Esmeralda.

"Depends. Do you mean us? Everyone?"

"Not sure. Both."

"Maybe I should get one of those Shervonian Pedal Shepherds. What do you think, Esmeralda M.?"

"Now, please explain, dear lady. Is your imagination really flying out of bounds?"

"No, I'm intact. Thoroughly. Didn't you see that electric car that was parked down the driveway from your friend's cabin when we left?"

"No. I missed it. I wonder if it belongs to that guy who isn't Dominick?"

"You mean that sensitive-browed guy? Yeah, I can just see that dolly-boy driving it and pushing its little pedals with those illustrious calves of his. Lots of extra charge on those straight-aways! He looked fit to me! You know, I've been wondering if it's a gimmick or if those pedals actually do help charge the battery."

"Why haven't I heard of this before? Hydrogen-fueled seems to be big news. Shervonian Pedal Shepherd? Are you pedaling me, Carmela?"

"Honest! You haven't been reading the right mags lately—last couple of months. Apparently, they're really taking off in LA. Hey, with that kind of traffic, who needs a fast car?"

"Who needs a fast car, period?"

"Well, Esmeralda, be thankful you haven't gotten hooked yet. Anyway, you know this whole saving the earth business—it will be ceaseless! Travel is but one area where we'll have to make compromises and the solutions won't come with the sunrise. But not knowing what to do doesn't mean people should give up.

"I can see it already—trendies, especially the yuppie mentalities, who consider environmentalism passé, unless exercise is involved that is. I can see a whole new university department—Environmental Fitness! Hold me back! Someone! Before I develop this stupid idea any further. This shouldn't have anything to do with trends, you know. Some things are timeless and concern has to be one of them." The pace of Carmela's words had been accelerating rapidly and she was now practically puffing for her own fuel of choice—air.

"I understand. So, Carmela, your role will be as the official spokesmodel for environmentalism."

"Caustic, Esmeralda, nothing more than caustic."

"Well, you should be allowed to give pep talks, among other jobs of course."

"I don't know. I still haven't gotten through to Harpreet, and I've tried for ages. We all have to keep doing it, though—encouraging others. Set an example. You communicate with your photos, girl."

"Yeah, that and the accompanying stories. I want to

take this one more step and become a photojournalist. You knew that, I assume. Maybe I'll even become a cinematographer and make one of those harsh documentaries. The truth has to be told. I just remember how Mr. Wintergreen once said something akin to 'progress for the well-being of the earth and its residents is the only real progress that exists anymore'."

"Yeah, I remember. I didn't really know what he meant then. Didn't think much about it."

"I didn't either at the time, but sometimes I do now. I heard someone say though, that the reason we're on this earth is to make advancements, discoveries and inventions."

"Things will change. We can't stop that. But redefining words is part of that change or advancement in our knowledge. What 'progress' will mean to us is an example of progression in our thinking—part of humankind's natural relationship with a changing earth."

"Carmela, did you come up with that on your own?"

"Well, you know, when you're like me...look! Moon-shadows! That's what those are, right?"

"Did you?"

"Trusted friend, even you I cannot tell."

"Okay. Whatever. I think progress means something different to each person. It has to be that way if we're all individuals. I wonder what it means to Savannah? Or say, Jayson? Anyhow do you know his first name? Wintergreen's. Is it Sandcastle?"

After a short silence, Carmela said, "I have no idea. Would be worth a good yelp if it was." She looked at her friend. "Esmeralda, do you remember how I told you that I based who I liked on how strange their name was? Did you know I was joking? I used to always act so flighty. I think I'm at last heading toward a Planet Earth landing though. The truth is I've always chosen my friends on how big their heart really is—deep inside that is."

"I kind of figured as much," Esmeralda said. "So, you perform CAT scans or ultrasound on us in our sleep? Measure our internal organs? How big is my heart?"

"Big enough, but certainly not as big as your voicebox. Now still that voice; I've always admired you because you've never been afraid to be yourself. You of the random acts of kindness, you can act as nice as you really are. Even when you're sarcastic we know you aren't serious. You have a way of letting us know that."

"You know, I have to admit, all this time I've felt like the proverbial fifth wheel. I'm surprised you admire me."

Carmela sputtered, "Hey, if it's Jayson's Bug it could use a fifth wheel." Shared memories of Jayson's degradable car called for a brief laugh.

"Well, I appreciate that I've been accepted as part of the group even though I'm no centerpiece," Esmeralda added.

"Take this—we don't fuss too much about the centerpiece at our table. You should know that. It's the variety and the pleasantness of the courses that makes this dinner party work." Carmela waited a minute before continuing, "Someday I might be as much of a sweetie as you. I'm afraid people might think I'm an ignoramus though. They might try to take advantage of me. I guess you're strong enough not to let what people might think get in the way. Am I right?"

Esmeralda reflected a moment. "I don't think about it much. Maybe I am ignorant. Hah! Actually, I'm not as kind as I should be. It's just that it's the kind side of me that people pick up on. Maybe it's this naive face of mine. I enjoy it when people assume I'm stupid or try to take advantage of me 'cause that's my cue to do something clever or give them a hard knowing look. It makes their sinister little eyes telescope into big round observatories. Leaves 'em speechless. Yeah! I'm the deliriously insidious Medusa in the guise of a pixie."

"Drastically funny, Esmeralda!" moaned Carmela.

"Okay, okay, I guess I just believe that in time people will sort out who they should and shouldn't listen to. I hope! Or is it when or how? Everyone has a message, right? We just have to figure out how to interpret those messages."

"Is that what Mr. Wintergreen meant when he said, 'Time isn't always our foe'?"

"I guess so. Maybe partly."

"I'm finally starting to appreciate that man." Then Carmela looked nowhere and slowly said, "Why is it that he has to behave like he's on a soapbox, though?"

They entered the tent, climbed into their sleeping bags and switched themselves off.

Hearing the diggings of Desdemona, two stiff and sluggish young women arose early Saturday morning, still eager to head for an adventure. After a Cornflakes breakfast (Carmela saved the empty package, hopefully just for recycling and not to use as her own personalized pulpit), they loaded up and found their trail. Heading up the hilly path, it didn't take long for them to discover that their backpacks carried more than a thread of burden. They took frequent breaks—quaffed some water and poured trail mix from their hands to their tongues. They spoke to each other and their pack-laden pup about their worries and their fears. They commented on how they didn't habituate to the forest smell, like they did to most aromas. It was still present and wonderful.

Esmeralda educated Carmela on the species she could remember. Together they looked in awe at Nature's plan—the wildflowers, the banana slugs, the brackets of fungus, the nurse-logs, the beards of lichen—and how the pieces came together in a symbolic, syncopated, sometimes symbiotic symphony, the swaying leaves a multitude of conductors leading together in synchronized time and with sympathetic harmony.

"Maybe perfection's not so bad!" said Esmeralda.

Carmela smiled but had nothing to add.

The two endeavoured to be rugged. The dog had no trouble. A little body of water that bordered between being a pond and a lake seemed a peaceful spot to set up camp.

The next morning they decided to leave their camping gear behind and take inventory of the area around the water. A short stroll to the other side, a little trail led away from the lake. Curiosity made their sore feet follow it. To Esmeralda there seemed to be a purpose to this mission, although she had no idea what it could be. Minutes later they passed what looked like a midden—a native burial site. Normally, this might have attracted their attention, even if just momentarily, but, without disturbing a thing, they steered around it while still generally moving forward. Desdemona walked in a particularly pert fashion as something was calling all three of them on and around the base of a small mountain. Then they realized what it was: a sound, muffled and reverberated by numerous cages of trees. Soon they could distinguish it as the pure white noise of a suddenly falling river.

When they reached the basin of the waterfall, which was not huge, but certainly big enough to marvel at, Desdemona satisfied herself with a short drink. The two already tired hikers were ready for more serious rejuvenation. The precocious day now radiated, saying "early summer," and the two knew their body odour could stun or perhaps even petrify a more fit traveller. Without hesitation, they started stripping down to their underwear. Suddenly, Esmeralda stopped with a jerk.

"Why do I get this drowning feeling that Mr. Blonde is going to appear?" she said. "Wouldn't that just be the cream in the casserole!"

Carmela continued undressing and said, "You know, Esmeralda Mrky, it does appear that you are prejudiced!"

Esmeralda looked around. The only person she could see was her friend who now was wearing a black body suit with a white skeleton's ribcage stitched to thc front. Esmeralda then stripped the rest of the way to her varicoloured underpants and bra. "Am not. Have I ever treated Jayson unfairly? It's just that blonde men are all conceited and cruel. It's a fact."

"How we base our impressions of a group on so few samples. I'm surprised you don't dislike all those who have blue eyes or are six feet tall. Have you ever considered times when, maybe, just conceivably, blonde men were okay? Kind? Helpful?"

"You think of a time, Carmela. Can you? 'Cause I'll bet you anything those times are rare as a, um...an April mosquito." She slapped her arm. "That stung. Besides, look at you. You speak of any 'cute' man as if he were an object. That's just as bad."

"Don't be a p.c. extremist, girl," said Carmela. "You know it isn't."

The conversation stopped there, for both women were startled by the sound of an approaching troop. A whistling troop. The sound got louder until footsteps could be distinguished from whistles.

"Elmer!" shouted one of the group. The rest of the band stood still, looking startled themselves.

"Why, it is Elmer Mrky!" came a second shout. "You really do like colours. You weren't lying!"

"Uh, y-yes," said Esmeralda. She had broken her promise to herself. She had let Julieanne intimidate her again. Still, she could not feel bad because there, grinning, was Savannah, standing gracefully, womanly, yet awkwardly in her own way.

Julieanne, thinner than before and strikingly healthy in her silver-grey hair, proceeded to introduce the other three travellers in her group—Avril, Margo and Cindy. Without pause, Carmela introduced herself and her dog to the group.

"Well, I'd sure like to know how this chance meeting came to be," Julieanne said. "We were just returning from pursuing our auriferous desires, the five of us. We do this every year—search for gold." Then she whispered, "We're the only ones who know where this one particular vein is. We just leave it, so we can find it in its full splendour the next year. The pleasure is in the discovery, don't you think?"

Esmeralda glanced at Savannah, who had just finished taking off all her clothes.

Carmela said, "You must want to shower too, Savannah! Wow! I wish I had your nerve."

"I wish I had the nerve to wear what you're wearing, Carmela-bones!" Esmeralda retorted for Savannah.

"Here's your swimsuit, dear," said Julieanne. "I figured you'd put one in your pack and there it was—right on top. Just in case someone else appears." Savannah put it on.

"These rocks are pretty scratchy. It'll protect your trunk if you slip," added Carmela. She turned to Esmeralda. "Still laughing at me? Yeah, well look at you, Ms. Mrky. I can't imagine where on earth you would have found those ugly tasteless things you call underwear!"

Stepping to the clear deep pool beneath the waterfall, Esmeralda cupped her hands tightly and filled them with shockingly cool water which was then splashed across Carmela's skeleton. Immediately Carmela and Savannah proceeded to capture handfuls of liquid ice to torment Esmeralda and each other. Opportunity called, and the three approached the falling water and let it tease them into putting parts of themselves in for a test of boldness and spunk.

Cross the frigid stepping stones to the shower of no
time,
Where all memories come together under the
heading of "one life."

Toes lifting upward from the sole straight toward the sky;
Away from biting stone to reach the homey warm
and dry.
Slowly relaxing downward to rock coating—slippery
wild.
In motion holding tightly like a salamander child.

Step in; be shrouded by thick foggy curtains of
uncertainty.
Soon surrounded by a long glass sheet of pure and
simple clarity.
Women-children come out, show the meaning of
prosperity.
Ensure friendship finds its niche within your minds'
eternity.

Watch limp droplets storm to thunderous oblivious
streams.
Quench your pine for exhilaration; lighten with the
present steam.
Drumming water will massage your bright clear
dragonfly wings.
Rise and fall in singing mist made by perchance
meetings.

Splash, sisters, play;
By day in imaginary dresses.
Soft sky voices will chime,
"You were meant for this time."
The horizon will hold your caresses.

Wonder, sisters, dream;

It's dark in your minds' deep recesses.
Your souls hide within;
Take them out for a spin,
As you try on your many fine dresses.

You've become the dancing dewdrops of daylight's alluring parade.
Peer behind the falls—the rocks' decor—you're wall puppets in the shade.
Diurnal maidens come be recharged by refracted light,
Shine through the misty prism when twilight turns to night.

After the rhythm's penetrated, loosened pain from inside passages,
And you've felt the cold fire burn your skin, steam rising sent your messages;
When it's time to leave, your thoughts rejoin you in a tumbling elation.
You have felt the kiss of Nature's bliss in an eclectic celebration.

"Oh, those cascading dresses suited you so well!" Julianne sighed, as the pale-skinned young women stepped out of the cold and perched themselves on warm chair-like crannies in the rocks. She stretched a towel across the shoulders of the three.

Esmeralda and Carmela watched Savannah as she stared alternately at the storming water and the nearby scenery.

"Th-the wat-t-terfall illusion," chattered Carmela. "T-try it!"

Esmeralda found herself intrigued by the way, after a good long stare at the waterfall, her mind would make trees, bushes, boulders or anything seem to grow by looking at them.

"Which way are you headed?" asked Margo.

Carmela answered, "We have to go back to our campsite—it's around by a lake over there. Once we have our gear packed we're heading back to the parking lot at Gordon Bay."

"We're heading for the parking lot too, but had planned on taking a different route. But if you don't mind, we'd like to hike with you. Right gang?" asked Julieanne.

All nodded their heads in agreement.

On the way back Carmela was eager to talk to Savannah. Esmeralda ended up conversing with the other four women.

"Did you get the letter from my mom? She sent one to the address I have for you in Arizona, oh, about a month or two ago," asked Esmeralda.

"No. I haven't been in Arizona since December. I decided to stay here after last Christmas along with Savannah. Samuel's been going to university in Victoria since September. I've been meaning to get in touch with your mom for some time—love to see the bird lady again."

"How about your husband? He didn't stay?"

Cindy interjected, "Best not to ask about Nils, dear."

"Oh, that's okay," said Julieanne. "His heart is still in his position down in Arizona. It's been a rough road for us. I got tired of all the years of feeling unsure. I needed a change and I'm always happier here than down there."

"Will you get back together with him? Or should I ask that?"

"I don't mind. I suppose there's a chance. Then, of course, there's my fantasy man. If I met him that could really put a kibosh on things." She released a girlish giggle.

"You mean you have a fantasy man, too? What's he like?"

"You really shouldn't have asked that one," said Cindy.

"Oh, yes, you should have, because I love to talk about that fascinating spirit. Here he is. Listen. He's a short rugged man with long salt and pepper hair and a thick dark mustache, aquiline features, that is eagle-like—a fairly large, downward hooked nose and small dark eyes. Sometimes he's Spanish, sometimes French, Portuguese or English. The intriguing thing about him is he's a sixteenth-century explorer who is quite ahead of his time—being in British Columbia already. But he gets caught in a time warp. Now he's really ahead of his time, or behind it!

"I am the first person he meets when he appears in our present world, and at first he acts assured, so strong. He doesn't have much time to talk to me for he sees me as a chatty flippant woman. It doesn't take long, though, for him to realize that he is the one who is out of place. He panics a bit. He is confused. I help him out by showing him the makings of today and explaining as much as I can about the present world. He finds me a proficient 'mentor of modern' and thinks I must be incredibly intelligent to understand so much about this strange new world he's experiencing.

"So impressed is he with my knowledge of the land that was to be his conquest—he's never heard of a female geologist before, although they must've existed in some form in his time and place, and he thinks I'm a pioneer. I try to tell him differently, but I'm not sure if he believes me. Then—"

Cindy interrupted, "You mean there's more to it? I haven't heard this part...."

"Then," Julieanne continued, "well, now he becomes a different man—a man seeking enlightenment instead of power. A gentle poet inhabits him. He says something deeply romantic, then I get to tell him that William Shakespeare said almost the same thing. And he says, 'William who?' And I explain. Then he says something quite clever, thrilling and mysterious, and I tell him that Edgar Allen Poe once said something akin to that. And he says, 'Did you introduce me to him?' And I say, 'No' and explain.

"Later, he says something too touching and I just have to inform him that he sounds like Longfellow, for in my fantasy I know all the works of all the famous authors. Anyway, he says, 'A very tall man, I presume!' only in his 16th-century way. I carry on and tell him all I know about Longfellow. An hour later I finish and with his chance to speak he says, 'As time moves by it gets more and more difficult to be original!' But I let him know he's an original!"

"Now you can go on!" exclaimed Avril.

"No, that's all there is. But actually I hope that I never meet such a man."

"Well, you know that you won't," said Margo. "But, why?"

"Because if he's as wonderful as I imagine, I will die of excitement and if he's not a thrill, then disappointment will be my demise."

Several groans came in unison.

"I have never felt so normal in my life!" said Esmeralda.

"Same here, honey, only with my life being so much longer than yours, I get a bigger exclamation point at the end!" said Cindy.

Esmeralda turned and looked behind her. "Savvy did you get the letters I wrote to you? I wrote about one a year. I got one letter back from you and then no more."

"Yes!" said Savannah.

"After she first wrote to you, I believe she received some questions from you. From then on she privately read your letters, then hid them in a drawer. She didn't think the rest of us should see them," said Julieanne.

"That's all right. She didn't have to write back. I'm

glad I had someone to write to 'cause otherwise my digits could've dulled. Understand there was a time I didn't do much in the way of homework. You know what, though, I was always disappointed that I didn't have any pictures of Savannah to look back on. I could always imagine her moving, but couldn't find a clear image of her face in my mind. We're almost back to our camp. I'll take bunches of pics of you people when we're there."

"I'm an artist—of a sort. I have several sketches of Ms. Savannah. I'll give you one sometime," Margo said.

"We need pictures of you, Esmeralda. We only have an old one. And, of course, your dear friend Carmela, too!" said Julieanne.

Back at the tentsite, a major camerafest took place as they packed.

Carmela whispered to Esmeralda, "You know what I really perceive about Savannah? She's so feminine! But in a natural way. It's like she doesn't put it on and she doesn't hide it—it's just there. I wish I could be like that."

Esmeralda whispered back, "She's just a natural in all ways. She's never tried to impress people; she just loves them. She's genuine, unique, in a sense untamed. Now you can see why she's such an inspiration."

On the way back to the parking lot Esmeralda and Carmela were convinced by a persistent Julieanne to spend the night at the dome cabin. Avril, Margo and Cindy would return to their own homes.

CHAPTER EIGHTEEN

SHATTERED

Back at the cabin, Julieanne had no trouble striking up a conversation with Carmela while Esmeralda and Savannah became reacquainted.

"Adorable dog! I can see why you brought your Gravity Defier along."

"Yeah. She's a beaut. Makes me feel safe, too." Carmela glanced at the mostly blank walls and asked, "What do you people do around here when you're not out gold-mining?"

"Well," answered Julieanne, "you might know that my daughter has this amazing nose. The scent of some perfumes can irritate her so, but some smells soothe. Together we decided to grow this big herb garden—just for fun. Of course, once you get one idea, it's hard to stop the others from rolling in and somehow we've started up this little herb business. We call it 'Savvy Savories.' I have a hard time stopping Savannah from packaging—she loves her work. We also make this great mix for 'herb cakes.' A dollop of basil, a dab of thyme, a pinch of oregano, but just a freckle of dill, all in a pancake-type mix. We'll make some for dinner in a minute. Not your traditional Easter dinner, but, after backpacking, almost anything tastes like a fine feast, right?"

"Do you grow many types of herbs?"

"Only about fifteen so far. I believe soon our little enterprise will move into dried flower arrangements and soap-making and who knows on what fantastic voyage of discovery that will lead us?"

"Is this a seven-days-a-week type pursuit? I mean on the days you're not travelling."

"Oh, never. I won't let Savannah work that hard. It's

hard for her to stop, but if she didn't she'd miss out on the other experiences she enjoys. I take her to her 'retreat'—three, four days a week, it's variable, actually. I tell her she needs a break from me—I'm not an easy person to live with."

Carmela disagreed, "Come on, you must be a real sweetie to put it that way. I bet you're wonderful with her. You have such a calm underneath your energy. Do you take yoga?"

"No, but I believe that if there is a God, that She—and, of course, God doesn't have to be a 'She,' it's just a habit of mine—She probably decided Savannah needed someone with low blood pressure. I'm proud to announce to the world that mine has gone up to 118 over 75. Used to be so low that I'd get lightheaded. Now I only seem that way."

"You're joking," said Carmela. "Are you really as confident as I think you might be? I can never tell about people. Tell me, please. I want to figure out confidence. It seems that whenever I reach the point where I feel I will be highly self-assured for the rest of my life, I suddenly talk myself out of it."

"That's Nature's way of keeping you in balance, dear. Confidence, when indestructible and pure, could be dangerous—could make you unsympathetic for one thing. Margo once said that having the correct dose of the attribute has kept her striving to improve her talent as an artist."

Julieanne continued, "However, I do, because I need it, pursue a higher level of confidence. You have to give yourself permission to do so. This may sound loco, but if I lose self-faith, I require myself to read a little pep talk I once wrote. Is it ever a nauseating piece. So I seldom lose confidence for I clearly don't want to have to read that terrible condescending fluff. If you want to, write your own. Just make sure it's something you never want to read again. If that doesn't work, when nobody's looking give yourself a huge embrace."

Julieanne turned her head. "Savannah, sounds like you're already getting Elmer to tell you stories. You do have that influential way about you."

"We were telling stories, but Savvy is now showing me some books. What's this? *A Snapshot of My Life*, by Savannah. Cool. This book's all about you. Look at that picture of you. Hilarious...'I love to jump on my rebounder, especially when it's snowing. I have to watch that I don't slip, though.' I'll say!"

Julieanne said, "Will you excuse me, young ladies? Just carry on. I'll be back momentarily."

Carmela walked over to have a look. "What are these other books? Hmm, this binder has 'Savannah Stories' written on it. Inside it's got stuff, I guess little fables about Savannah and how she does things. Wow, you do a lot Savannah. Here you are at a restaurant. In this one you must be going to the movies. 'I remember to use my quietest voice at the theatre,' it says. Look at all these stories about you!"

"I write stories on the computer," said Savannah.

"Which book is that?" said Carmela.

"That one and that one and that one and that one," Savannah answered, pointing as quickly as she spoke.

Esmeralda picked one up and started reading. " 'Once there was a Mr. Magoo who ate three pizzas for dinner and Rocky came and offered some Trident gum, recommended by dentists for when you can't brush and Preparation H is doctor-recommended, but we do not talk about that when we are at the restaurant. We have to use our good language at school and at the store and at home and everywhere and sometimes Savannah likes to scream, but Savannah really likes to talk about characters and go to the playground and kick soccerballs with Rocky and Bullwinkle. Then the big wolf came and—' "

Savannah said, "I had a boyfriend."

"Oh," said Carmela. "And he is not your boyfriend anymore?"

"He is not my boyfriend anymore. He got mean. Julie says if people get mean I should tell them to take a hike. I told him to hike all the way around the island and then climb to the top of Mount Washington and then take the ferry and hike around another island. That will take a long time." Savannah popped out of her chair and said, "Washroom," and ran off.

"Better pause the story for her," said Carmela as she turned to Esmeralda. Then she said, "I keep forgetting to ask what you think of Garyd's girlfriend."

Esmeralda screwed up her face. "What? Garyd has a girlfriend?" She tried to hide her slight disbelief and the minuscule hint of jealousy and sadness that rocketed through her system, but as she asked "So what's she like?", a combined expression of relief and dejection pushed through her skin and reached Carmela.

Carmela responded, "Sorry, I thought you were there when we met her. What is she like? Well she's not terribly scenic, if you know what I mean, but she's worldly in a kind way, and somehow Garyd knows this; he treats her as though she's fresh off heaven's boat—the angel queen."

Just then Julieanne returned, followed by Savannah. "It's always great to hear they're still making gentle-men. So, shall we...oh, what do we have here on the end table? An envelope? Good-sized." She picked it up. "Unopened. How did this get here? It's from Nils."

Esmeralda looked around and sensed a kind of reverence on each face, including Savvy's. She was surprised when Julieanne opened the envelope and started reading a letter aloud, but in a whisper:

My Dearest Julianna:

I realize that I've never written you a love letter in the 29 years I've known you. It seems odd, since I like to write and I love you immensely and completely.

Still after all these years and all the hard times and

all my stupidity, you are the only one for me. I know I'm a stuffy old codger, but you bring life to my soul, even though it doesn't always show. I will try to show it.

Please forgive my selfishness and impatience and my closed mind. I want to retire early, but only if you will be with me. Accept my gift—a poem for you, Julianna. It took a long time to write, because I wanted to get it right, but I'm not much of a poet and it probably isn't original, but please read the love in it:

If I were the ground, you would be the zephyr—
touching me—
sometimes tickling, sometimes soothing, stroking my soul.
If I were the sky, you would be the light—
in all its hues—
illuminating me, giving me variety,
letting me see so many views.
If I were the sea, you would be the oxygen—
moving throughout me—
giving life to all that lives within.

I remember walking by the night ocean with you and four tiny feet.
Invisible waves crashing, miniature flecks of light shining off farther waters.
A moving pincushion. And I was on needles and pins.
Something calling me.
Filling me with a desire for more.
How could I have wanted more?

I will keep writing poems for you, Julianna, until you ask me to stop or want me back, and if you do want me, I will still write poems, but they will be of joy. The odds were against us, but we made it a long, long way. Let's make it the rest of the way.

I now ask myself, 'Why is it that the women we find the most interesting, we try too hard to impress?' We either end up putting them down or turning them off. The last thing I wanted to do was lose you. I thought you liked it when I was stoic, but I was wrong. I'm so sorry, lovely lady.

I miss your craziness. I miss your thoughtful smile. I miss debating all those trivial details. I miss you.

I must go now so that I can write letters to my children. I have so much to say to them, too. You will be hearing from me in a short while.

Forever,
Nils

P.S. Enclosed are some letters that showed up for you.

"I do believe this will be the year that I learn to truly, passionately, love poetry," sighed Julieanne. Then she looked up, saw the three young women staring at her and blushed a little.

"Will you take him back?" asked Carmela.

"I wouldn't mind a few similar letters first," Julieanne smiled. "A kind man though, he really is. Especially when I think back—when I was so so young and so confused and getting into big trouble, headed for worse. I had less common sense than most people my age, but thought I had more. I met Nils and thought him odd, so studious, but he cared enough about me to save me from what I thought was a destiny of doom. And how could I not fall in love with him? He gave me such a big chance when he was full of aspiration and life. Now I must give him a chance—sometimes I feel like I've stolen some of that life out of him—I'll give some back, if possible, and we can be on equal ground."

The four women proceeded to whip together a batch of herb cakes for their dinner. At one point Savannah gave Julieanne a big hug and kissed her on the cheek. Julieanne seemed touched. Savannah thieved a cake from the serving plate and laughed all the way to the table.

"I know you're smarter than me. Do you have to keep rubbing it in?" Julieanne said, but Esmeralda could not tell if she was being serious or jocular.

As they set the table Savannah fell into what seemed like a regular routine: "And now let's have a big hand for our first contestant, all the way from the farm, it's Butter!"

A "Yay!" and a clap came from Julieanne.

"And now, ladies and gentlemen—"

"All the way from Quebec," Julieanne interjected.

"We have our next contestant, Maple Syrup. Let's have a big round of applause for our competitors!"

Everyone clapped and cheered and merrily devoured the herb cakes.

After the disappearance of the feast, Esmeralda turned to Savannah and said, "There's something I have to show you, Savvy. It's in Carmela's car. I'll be right back."

When Esmeralda returned she had something in her hands, wrapped in paper towelling. She removed the carol sphere and held it up before Savannah's eyes.

"This helped me write stories—for my letters."

Savannah, open-mouthed, reached for it with both hands. Esmeralda moved the sphere into her fingertips, but let go a fraction of a second too early. Her reflexes in action, Savannah bobbled it with surprising quickness, but really had no chance, and the carol sphere fell onto the wooden floor and crashed and smashed into many tiny and large splinters. Savannah screamed. Julieanne let out an "Oh, no!"

Savannah ran, wailing, to her bedroom.

Esmeralda wanted to follow, but Julieanne suggested that she give her a minute. A broom and dustpan were spotted by Carmela, who calmly swept up the broken glass. Staring at the pieces as they were hoisted away, Esmeralda knew that the sadness she felt had little to do with the cherished object itself, but more with what the sphere had brought to her and what it meant to Savannah.

Carefully she shuffled to Savannah's room. She found her sitting in a chair in the corner, clenching something, one hand inside the other, saying, "You have to sit in the quiet chair, you've been naughty. Naughty, naughty, naughty young lady. Now take this you dirty rat stick and stop your wild sniffing. Both of you. Do you hear me?"

"No, Savvy, you weren't naughty. It was my fault that it dropped. I'm sorry. But, you know what? That ornament was only special to me because it reminded me of you and how you always gave me permission to tell stories—any kind of story that stumbled into my head. I could tell it any way it came, any way I wanted, and you would love it because it was a story and it was me. Maybe it was even my way of speculating, that is trying to imagine, what kind of magic lives within your world. What you see. I don't know. I'll never know your world."

Savvy stared at her dresser, straight in front of her. Esmeralda sat beside her. She did not need eye contact to sense that Savvy was listening. Savvy, quiet now, would pick up the image she needed and more through her peripheral vision—a strength Esmeralda remembered well. Questions arose in her mind. *When Savvy looked into a glass ornament was she really absorbing nothing that was straight ahead and an enormous circus in the periphery? Or was she watching the dances that reflected themselves upon hitting the glass? Or a marvelous centrepoint her imagination could create?* This could not be dismissed.

"Now it is time for me to tell you...please believe me Savvy. I don't need it anymore. The sphere. I have seen you again. I have pictures of you. Besides, I now understand that your permission will always be within me. I can do whatever I think is right, say whatever I believe, imagine whatever I want, look for the answers that will bring more questions to mind—and it's because of you. I would be less of a person now if I hadn't known you. Did you know that?"

"Yes!" answered Savannah, practically recovered. As she had in the past, she swirled her thumb around and up. Then she opened her right hand to reveal a piece of turquoise. Esmeralda felt certain it was the same piece that had been part of the earring—the one she had given Savannah years ago.

Quickly, Esmeralda pointed her thumb straight toward the ceiling.

"I'm sure you would have been a wonderful person either way, Esmeralda." Julieanne stood at the door, smiling serenely. "It was always in you. You couldn't help it."

"I don't know if that's true," said Esmeralda.

"Actually, there is no way for me to know either," said Julieanne. "Will you visit us now and then, dear? Your mom and dad, too? Bring them along."

"That's my plan, but you people have to come see us, too."

"I'm sure we will. Now Savannah, would you like us to leave you alone, so you can rest? You've had quite the day, precious angel."

"So have you, Julie. Sweet dreams. I will have a little snooze now," answered Savannah She placed the turquoise on her nightstand.

"Tell you more stories tomorrow," said Esmeralda as she left the room.

Savannah quietly sang, "The Curveplane L visitors will run the triathlon after eating too much chocolate, oh yes they will, so they will get on a triangle instead of a bicycle, because they looked for an answer, oh yes they will, and dance with their guitars in India of old, oh yes they will, and Savvy will learn like Elmer and Savannah will grow up to be a beautiful woman, just like Esmeralda…"

CHAPTER NINETEEN

JUDGMENT DAYS

As Julieanne led Esmeralda back to the kitchen, they passed Carmela, collapsed and asleep on the same pastel paisley couch that Julieanne had turned to "Jell-O" on years ago. They covered Carmela with a blanket and made a pot of homegrown lavender-mint tea.

Julieanne stared at Esmeralda's baffled expression, surmising that she was struggling to find the right question to ask.

"You know, I think my children helped me just as much as my husband—developing my common sense. I had to learn quickly. As a baby Savannah was so bright and energetic, so much more alert than the other babes. In her second year she regressed. We were thrown astray, needless, well...."

She glanced around the room. "I think back at what a great mother I was when those two were little. Great, yet far from perfect. I'm not a bad mother now though, but I just don't really feel like a mother. More like an actress. And I've played the role so many times that I've got it down to a light breeze. I blow gently in and out of their being." Julieanne swallowed loudly. "Nils once said that he didn't understand how I made it through so much without going crazy. I just laughed, as I usually do, and said that I *had* gone crazy but he just hadn't accepted it. He thought I was so amusing. He didn't know I was close to being serious." She poured the tea, slowly inhaling its steam.

"What was the hardest thing for you? As a parent that is," Esmeralda acted like a talk show hostess. Julieanne managed to keep herself from laughing.

"Other people. That was an easy one—you'll have to find more challenging questions than that. People love to stare when they think you can't see them. They don't seem to know about peripheral vision or that we can actually hear them when they are behind us. The sincere looks and questions don't bother me; it's the rude comments and dirty looks that eat you. And, oh, I love the ones who assume that because we have a child with a disability we must be disabled too.

"Most people are quite understanding though, it's just a few. My favourites are the ones who believe it's our fault the girl has autism. Terrible parenting it must be. So they give you lots of advice. We're either too lenient or too strict. We don't yell at our child enough; we don't give her enough independence; we don't pay enough attention to her. They don't notice the child who is making it through just fine. That child's invisible.

"And you know what? You believe these things sometimes because you so want to have answers. And it takes years to completely stop blaming yourself. You can come up with a thousand things you might have done to cause the problem, as much as you know it probably had nothing to do with your actions: you dressed her too warmly, you didn't sleep enough when pregnant, you tried to cuddle her too much, sang the same song over and over too many times, or read the same book, you didn't have enough visitors when she was a baby, you had too many visitors—I think you get the gist.

"As Savannah grew up I constantly heard new words, with such terms as 'hyperlexic' and 'Asperger's' and 'Lovaas' becoming regular parts of our vocabulary. I sometimes hoped that she'd be one of those so-called 'recovered autistics' we hear about, but it hasn't happened—though we see the occasional evidence of progress. I think she's trying. 'Have we missed anything?' we often ask. We've tried a number of suggestions, but no magic solution has come into our grasp. A new prescription; I imagine it will be awhile before we have the medication issue figured out. Love works the best of anything—without it all our lives would be miserable. How can I put this? Gosh," she paused, then emphasized each word as she spoke, "It is hard to watch someone who has a hard time showing the world some of the best things about herself."

Esmeralda stared, as if thinking, *Tell me more.*

"The other tough part was early adolescence, before we met you. Age eleven—impossible. I didn't think we'd make it. Nobody forewarns you about this and as far as I know there's not much documented on it, but I would bet that almost any parent of an adult with autism will tell you how adolescence is magnified in these people. The hormone surge absolutely frustrated Savannah into a monster so unlike herself. Cinderella and Mr. Hyde's more evil twin sister battled it out in a bottle, which was her body, and the victor could not be predicted. Obviously, things got better."

"Who deserves the most credit for helping her progress? Would it be you?"

"There are so many people who would like to take credit and there are many who are too modest, and really most of them deserve some measure of that huge compliment, but at the same time Savannah is the unique and lovely candle they all added a little warmth to. Now her flame is bright and should last a long time. I hope."

"Are you glad that she was your child? You always seem to be."

"When phrased that way, honey, yes, because we always loved her and tried our hardest and knew she was best off with us. We all learned so much from having her around. Open-mindedness comes to my head, acceptance, patience, an appreciation for looking at things differently. It was a tough adventure, but such trips can be enjoyable if you take them in short enough legs—piece by piece, and if you don't let a desire for perfection destroy you. I've met so many kind-hearted people because of Savannah, I certainly can't complain about that. I honestly have to add, though, we had it much easier than some families. She is fairly high-functioning, especially in a social sense, and has such a wonderful disposition. You probably know there's no archetype; people with autism vary from each other just as much or maybe even more than the rest of us vary from each other."

Julieanne looked at her slippers. "'The rest of us,' I can't believe I said that. I suppose I see autism as more of a continuum, with most people having some degree of it, valuable all, but I don't know if I'm right. I have so many of these theories."

"Like…?"

"How about that autism relates to an inability to distinguish recent memories from old ones. Or information. A blending of long- and medium-term. Is that why when asked a question Savannah will often offer an answer from something way back? 'What did you eat for lunch?' 'Perogies.' 'That was two months ago, hun.' Distant events may seem recent to her—her memory is so good. Does it have to do with her senses being so powerful? They're always conjuring up memories from the past that interfere with the present. Often I wonder if there's too much interference from her acute perceptions. Maybe she doesn't become accustomed, as the rest of us do, to smell or other things she senses. She needs to stimulate herself to block out the overload she's perceiving. Does she have little faith in cause and effect? Is it a biochemical problem? Neurological?"

"Could it be both?" asked Esmeralda.

"Maybe. Or maybe someday we'll learn that autism is caused by a chemical imbalance and Asperger's has to do with damage to a small area of the brain, or vice-versa, and that these two causes produce some similarities. Who knows? Some say high-functioning autism and Asperger's are really the same thing.

"Sigh! Some of my theories have been encouraged or donated by other parents, and some, even though I thought of them, I can't remember—I guess I really am different from Savannah. There's the theory that has to do with unevenness in perceiving time. Then, one day I got to thinking that perhaps autism is only Mother Nature's little safety valve against the human race unfolding, developing too far. Allergies, viruses, bacterial infections, immune system abnormalities, immunization reactions, early ear infections—is this a cause or is it, along with autism, a result of an unusual ear structure?

"I would tell you about my theory of autistic relativity if only I could develop it. It'd put all of Einstein's theories to shame. I call each new idea the 'Theory of the Day,' even though they're not that frequent. To make sense out of all these ideas is difficult indeed. I sometimes have to remind myself not to worry so much about the cause, and get on with it. But what if I found a solution? Not likely, but...." Her words now sounded dreamy, "I wish I could be one of those incredibly wise women of few words."

"Do you think part of her brain works too fast—that another part can't assimilate all the information? Her body sure moves quickly."

"Someone else said something like that and suggested she take Tai Chi. She's signed up for a class that starts soon. We'll give it a try. I wonder how the instructor will do."

"It's so fascinating, Julieanne. She really is lucky to have you."

"People admire me. People pity me. They look at me with awe. Look at me with sorrow, even disdain. See me as different because of this zest I convey which is really a survival tool. I'm just human, though. It could have happened to someone else's kid instead. How can people be so judgmental, so self-righteous? I sure learned that you need to report any little bruise to the school, any scrape, because if they notice first, they might get suspicious. Protecting children is important, but somehow they target the wrong families." She cast a thoughtful glance at a spider waiting patiently in a web on a ceiling corner. "Most any challenge that comes my way now will seem easy."

"I can see why!"

"Now, if you had phrased your earlier question differently, Esmeralda; if you had asked me if I was glad that she had this challenge, I would have given you an emphatic 'no.' And the only reason I say this is because I ask myself if I would rather be what they call 'autistic' or not. And I would choose not to, even though it could be a fascinating world; it would be so hard, too hard. So how could I wish that on my daughter? I look at my son and I'm so thankful that he didn't have to go through what she did.

"Interestingly, if you don't mind me carrying on, I recently heard a geneticist say that a cure for autism could be coming within a decade. At first I could only think of this as wonderful, of course, but then comes a fear and all kinds of questions. Side-effects? Would she be happy? How long would it take to see changes? What would the transition be like for her? For us? I wish I knew which way she herself would rather be. Maybe someday she'll be able to tell me; she continues to improve her ability to communicate. I try picturing her without autism. How I'd love to carry on a long conversation with her. Still, I would miss the old Savannah."

"Autism doesn't really change who she is down deep. She'd still be basically the same person, wouldn't she?"

"I don't know. I even wonder which way's best for society. So many plusses and minuses of varied and shifting values, mostly unknown. Who's a good enough mathematician to solve that equation?" Julieanne took a long sip of tea and said, "Thank you, Esmeralda. I've never said all that to anyone before. I won't need to say it to anyone again. You're quite the gifted listener."

To Esmeralda's surprise, Julieanne pulled something small from her blouse pocket and placed it in Esmeralda's hand. "I came upon this one day—the match to the turquoise earring. It should be with you."

Esmeralda took a close look, for it was getting dark, but she could tell that, indeed, this was similar to the earring she had given Savannah. She looked at Julieanne while combing her mind for words, eventually saying, "I have a special place, my pouch, where I will keep this."

Julieanne had already found the words she desired, "I think it will be fascinating when the day comes that I look back on all the thoughts I just shared and they will seem primitive. We will know so much more. But for now, Slumberland calls this worn woman. Crash when you like."

CHAPTER TWENTY

IRIDESCENCE

An active mind, one that has just listened and learned and is now coming to its own conclusions, cares not to induce sleep upon itself.

Esmeralda silently strolled to the dock, to its end and sat, dangling her bare blistered toes in and out of the numbingly cold water. *Are smart people more sensitive? I don't know.* The lake sparkled. Leaves and grass rustled, nudged by a mild wind. A raven stood on alert in a cedar, sounding goose-like. The smell of algae once again became apparent. *What would I be like if I were more sensitive? A little more so? Way more so?*

She thought about the notion of success and realized that one could not argue against using that term to describe Savannah—she was happy and peaceful. And at peace. She engaged herself in activities that brought her joy. *How could one ensure this continued for her?*

As Esmeralda watched the sun set over the hills—monuments to the sculpturing of the lake—she remembered being on top of one of the peaks with Savvy, Julieanne and Maxine one warm summer eve years ago while on a camp-out, enticed while watching the sunset from up high, and appeased. Presently, she looked up at the sky. Stars were making their appearance, one by one. She focused on the star she thought might be Polaris:

Long ago the stars, galaxies and all phenomena visible in the celestial sphere had entertained Savvy and Esmeralda on several warm clear nights. As they lay on their backs in the field by their houses, Esmeralda watched her friend slowly move her head back and forth. When she tried doing the same, she discovered that it looked as though she were rapidly moving through space. The two girls moved their heads faster, then stood up and ran in circles, first large, then smaller and smaller, all the while looking up at the sky, until sky and land blurred together and they landed in a clump of tall grass.

They made sure they landed gently because now they were cosmic researchers who knew exactly what they were doing. "Khryslilion," a planet of mysterious transformations, was where they had landed.

Explorations needed to be done. Experiments to be performed. A maple tree was their spaceship. The full moon was their flashlight. The girls spent a great deal of time renaming species and developing new descriptions of the activities of the specimens they found. Many minutes were spent looking at iridescent beetles under the moonlight. Then ground control called them back to earth.

"Get your crazy britches in the house, you lunatics!" called Samuel the Lizard Boy. "Mom's been wondering where you two were!"

CHAPTER TWENTY-ONE

AGAIN

Esmeralda heard the quiet rumble of a car pulling up to the house. As her mind left the sky and the memory and returned to the lake, she became hypnotized by what appeared to be the water's reflection of the stars. She recalled something Julieanne had said about Nils not being able to train himself to block out the excess noise. Julieanne had to let herself "space-out" if she were to survive, because she could not quiet her daughter "more than a hundred times a day." All most people could do to "help" was to remind her that her life would not be an easy one. Julieanne, however, had made it. Maybe because she had little choice.

Still in her own space, Esmeralda barely paid attention to the sounds of a cabin door opening and closing, a bark that quickly stopped, and a subsequent opening and closing again. A few minutes later, the dock wiggled slightly. Slowly Esmeralda turned her head around. It was the blonde man. He squatted beside her and said a quiet "hi." She looked straight into his kind brown eyes and immediately envisioned two hazelnuts hovering in a field. Shortly, the hazelnuts turned into two children, laughing, running through the dry overgrown grass.

"Hello, Samuel," she said. She was surprised only by the fact that she had not been thrown into shock.

"You remember me! It's funny, I thought Mom was half asleep when she called out, 'Be quiet Desdemona,' and murmured something about you being out here. But it is you." He smiled his same mischievous smile, but his voice held glee. He looked much like the man in the sphere, with all his imperfections perfectly placed, but he was different too—a tad more baby-faced, and, although height was something she paid little attention to, she felt he was shorter than expected. He nearly lost his balance as he took off his shoes at the end of the dock and as he sat down beside her Esmeralda took her turn wearing an impish grin. The thought that this man might be clumsy was a welcome one. He was human.

Esmeralda's voice moved up an octave. "I now remember seeing you in the Funky Quarter, several years ago. I stared at you because I thought you looked familiar, then looked away because I thought I was being rude. That must've been around the time of the rock concert."

"Whitmore and I were in Vancouver for the Outrageously Normal concert. I saw you too. Savannah had told me where you worked and I said I would stop by and see how you were doing. I had just become certain that it was you with the mile-long ponytail when you disappeared to the kitchen and you didn't come out again. I asked the pierced waitress and she said you'd just finished your shift and were gone."

"You left the oak tree brooch?"

"My aunt gave us each one. It's a birthstone family tree. I remember that Savvy is the diamond, makes sense since she's the diamond in the rough, and my mom is green and my dad is red. Or maybe it's dad who's green and mom who's red. Mine, I believe, was the turquoise-coloured one. I just remember my stone was cool, but less regal. Anyhow, I thought I would keep with the tradition of our youth and give it to you."

"Tradition?"

"Yeah. Besides, I felt embarrassed about having women's jewelry hiding in my room."

"Do you want it back? Now that you're older and presumably less embarrassed."

"No, please keep it."

They both looked at the water for several minutes. Esmeralda seemed engulfed by her thoughts.

Samuel said, "Then there was that time we caught you for a second at the bus stop by the restaurant." He broke into an unexpected sermon:

"That term, 'politically correct,' has become the flavour. So often a complaint and so often an excuse for not getting involved.

Nobody wants to be called a p.c.—a label overused to the point that its meaning has become unclear. It's fine to be aware of it, I suppose, and not go overboard on being a goody-goody, but do you get the feeling the teeter totter is about to hit ground?

Why don't we broaden the fulcrum to create an even plane, then leap off from wherever we're sitting, first one foot and then the other onto this planet's soft soil, timeline-fine, and just do what is correct without the 'political' in front of it? Do what's best and stop using so much energy complaining about each other. I believe your generation will do it. You are media-literate, right? Don't let them defeat you and your confidence. And with the thinks and the knowledge you possess, extremists will no longer irritate others to a nonsensical opposition or apathy.

Follow your hearts, for your generation may be the best ever. Love, love of humanity and the earth will guide. I sense that a new era of harmony has come with you young ones. Not many know that yet, but, you are so fortunate."

"Who does that remind you of?" Samuel asked.

"A musician? Visitors from another dimension? No, a Savvy recitation!"

"No, Mr. Wintergreen said almost exactly that to us. I remember it so well. Never heard someone so adamant."

"Oh, you met him? Obviously."

"Both times we ate at your restaurant."

"What did you think of him?"

"Opinionated but nice. He's the one who told me that if I wanted to write children's stories I should do it." He thought a moment, then continued in his young, soft but masculine way, "Did you know that I used to spy on you all the time? To hear your stories, I'd sneak up when you were entertaining Savvy. Or when our moms had me hide money or gems for you and Savvy to find, sometimes I'd kind of have to stick around awhile. Wished I could make things up like you could. I know I teased you sometimes, but I really emulated you.

"Now I realize I was a little worried that Savvy liked you better than me. I told her stories, and still do, but I never thought they were as good as yours were. Mr. Wintergreen said that we can't make up each other's stories. People have their own set of stories to create and relate. We may love our own stories, but we'll always be in awe of another's ability because it's different from our own." His eyes surveyed some nearby trees. "You must know, if you still work there—did he save up enough to make it back to visit his homeland? Ghana, I think?"

"Not sure, but I'll ask him." Then she asked, "So will you become an author?"

"Yes but probably as a hobby. I haven't decided yet whether I want to concentrate on becoming a writer, a librarian or a teacher. I'm considering Special Ed., but Mom warns me against it, saying that I've already put in my time. I love reading and telling stories to kids. When I worked at a daycamp last summer I used to tell traditional stories, only I'd change the roles around so the kids could see how ridiculously stereotypical some of them were—you know, old instead of young, races reversed, female instead of male—that kind of thing. They loved it. Sometimes I get carried away, though. Have you ever heard of Pooch in Boots?

"No. Try another on me."

"Let's see. How 'bout the saga of Big Blue Boy Riding Hood who visited his uncle who had the gout and on the way was harassed by a power-hungry female toad?"

"Haven't." She looked at his nose. "Have you ever done a role-reversal on Beauty and the Beast?"

"No, but it would most likely be enlightening."

"Too close for me! Oh, I forgot—I shouldn't say things like that. I hope to write, too, but in a different vein."

"Oh, yeah?"

"I need to write factually, because I need to tell the world the truth about what is happening. My photos will validate my words."

"Can you be completely truthful? Can anyone?"

"They say what we consider to be the facts are only what we perceive of them. Photographs, like anything else, rely on interpretation and can be deceitfully in love with camera angle, focus, point of reference, the tint of the lens... The most honest attempt at truth is what we must pursue. Bet that sounds memorized." Esmeralda paused, then gave him a wicked glare. "How honest is your fiction?"

"Eerily." Samuel glared back at her. "It's amazing how much truth you can get away with hiding within fiction. It's there for those who will accept it, to be interpreted in each reader's most honest way. I heard that somewhere."

As Samuel pulled his feet out of the water, Esmeralda found herself staring, for the baby toe on his right foot was practically gone; just a stub of dead-looking skin appeared. This she did not remember.

"Wondering about my toe? That's okay. I don't mind. Many a stupid thing I have done and hopefully less are to come. Frostbite. Thirteen years old. We skied too far. Let ourselves get overtired. Whitmore probably saved me from worse. Fortunately I was small for my age and he was able to piggyback me the last half-kilometer after I tore a ligament. It's not a pretty sight or story. A girlfriend broke up with me when she saw my foot."

"You're not serious!"

"I am. Guess she wanted indefectibility. Good thing I got rid of that shallow thing early in the game."

"How could someone be such a flake?" She now realized how wonderfully far from perfect he was.

"Listen to this. Another girl, dear Natasha, dumped me like compost after she met my family. And Mom was even on her best behavior. From now on they see the foot, they meet the family—first month. No exceptions."

"Those were unreal girls, Samuel. Do you have a girlfriend, now?"

His cheeks gradually reddened as he answered, "No, I'm young and I plan on waiting until I meet someone, and, who knows, maybe I have already, someone who will love me even if I get in a terrible accident and get my face rubbed off. The problem is I seem to attract the wrong type. Whitmore says my hair is too nice. Says I need to go get myself a 'bad haircut.' Then the good-hearted, the genuine ones will regard me. I told him that the problem with bad haircuts is they grow out so darn fast and then look half-decent and you just have to keep chopping at it, which isn't something I want to have to worry about." His handsome face was now screwed up repulsively.

Esmeralda giggled. "Who is this Whitmore, anyway?"

"You don't remember? You know Whit! My cousin?"

"No, didn't meet that one."

"Yes, you did. He remembers you. He thought you were so nice to give him your umbrella. All he could find to give you was his spare guitar pick." He thought a moment. "Oh, yes, Spider! He always went by 'Spider'!"

"You mean that scarved vagabond at the bus stop was Spider? That's why I have a guitar pick? You wouldn't believe what my imagination was doing trying to solve that mystery. Well, how is he?"

"Not at his best. He's had some problems. Such a great guy, but he can't keep out of trouble. Can't say no to temptation. Doesn't help that he works night shift at a convenience store. Meets some strange animals. Wants to play in a band, but never finds a good fit. You know what? I'm heading back to Victoria tomorrow and I'm going to see if I can convince Whit to find another job. Do you want to come along? He'd love to see you. We can stay at his parents' place. Lots of extra rooms. Just stay out of Diamanta's path. She probably hasn't changed much since you last saw her. Overprivileged. Won't give dust to Whit or anyone associated with him. You know what else? While we're there I—"

"I'm sorry, but I have to head back to my job tomorrow. I'll definitely be returning here though. I want to sit on this dock this winter so I can see if the light of the December Pleiades reflects off Cowichan Lake. Watch the winter seeds of red, blue and green."

"Your mom used to say something like that when she gave us a gem to hide."

"Grow to winter gardens, seeds?"

"That was it."

"The Winter Carol. It lives in her year round. Sigh! Wait! That gives me an idea; I'll work on some tales about the seven sisters for Savvy." Esmeralda paused a minute and looked back at the cabin. "Oh yeah, my friend, Carmela, she has to head back to the mainland too. She's the one on the couch."

"And all this time I was wondering how Grace Slick got on our chesterfield. Stranger things have happened here, though."

"Grace Slick? Was she that Jefferson Airplane woman? Carmela's more like a big-boned Sheryl Crow, wouldn't you say? So, how do you know about Grace Slick?" As Esmeralda started to smile it looked like her whole face was cracking through her false scowl.

"Who says I knew? Just a name that popped into my head. You must know though. No, we'd better not go into this, something tells me. I remember what we went through over Santana. Then they went and made a comeback in 1999. I'm not so sure the world is ready for the return of Grace."

"You're right, Lizard."

Then it happened. They found themselves in the middle of a lengthy conversation about the past, something Esmeralda could not have predicted. Excitedly, they put together many of the pieces of the laminated puzzle of old times at the lake. This came before that. Who was with whom? Did I really say that?

"So, I have a sudden hankering for some s'mores," said Samuel. "Can I bring a round? I can check the cellar; do you have a chocolate preference? Dutch? German? Belgian…?"

"You're the connoisseur, no doubt. I'll trust your expertise."

"I won't ask you for a vintage."

"Wise." Then she whispered, "Ah, a man who will confess a love for chocolate, yet will share his with another. Could it be that I have misjudged." She looked at him. "Sorry."

His eyes smiled, but his mouth, with sucked-in cheeks, could not hide his slight embarrassment. "You stay here and enjoy the lake. I'll be back," he said.

Esmeralda did not mind waiting. Not on such a beautiful night. She thought about how easy it was to talk to Samuel now and she thought about the now, the present. *What is the present? Something fuzzy or something clear? Is it this day? Hour? An instant pinprick so fast that by the time you realize what it is it is gone?*

Whatever it was it was wonderful, she realized, then thought some more. She thought about how a worrier has tomorrow to worry, a doer has a better day to get things done, and how this is unlike procrastination, for the remarkable present of a remarkable present has to be lived if life is to be life. To be a carol.

From the kitchen the sound of Samuel's whistling, a tune with a randomly generated melody, reached Esmeralda's ears and she wondered about him. Again. *Does he ride a horse? Play guitar as well?* For all she knew he played the trumpet in a mariachi band. *Will I ever waltz to the sky with him? Will he ever kiss my hand?* Someday these questions might be answered; time aplenty for that. But right now it mattered little. For this was the present. So fine.

With full arms, Samuel quietly walked out of the house and over to a place of many campfires of the past. As he proceeded to crumple newspaper, he said, "Your friend Carmela has quite the snore!" He moved on to arranging kindling over the paper.

"Carmela? Yeah, sorry. Should've warned everyone."

"Not to worry, we're used to loud noises at night. Did Julieanne warn you about Savannah's singing?"

"No. It wouldn't have surprised me, though. I heard her sing, but quietly, tonight. Wait a minute. She did that as a kid, too!"

He lit a match and momentarily looked into it before putting the flame to the paper. "Sure did."

"And you're sure it was my mom that was responsible for all the treasures?"

"Both our moms—mostly. The turquoise earring was an accident—Julieanne lost it when she first toured your place, but wanted you to keep it. Afterwards it became a game for the two of them. They would spy on Whit and me as we spied on you and hid things. Us giving you the guitar pick and the brooch, they knew nothing about."

He put a piece of wood on top of the burning kindling. "Ah, fire's going. So, marshmallows—medium-rare—does my memory prove right?"

"You're warm. I mean you're right. Absolutely!"

"Me? I prefer those devils burnt and crispy. Brings out the best in the chocolate."

Esmeralda stood up on the dock. As she readied herself to join Samuel at the fire, she took one more look at the lake, the land and the entire vista.

Again, the jewel-emblazoned waters glistened. The wind softly blew the fragrant whispering grass.

Tanis Morran lives in Victoria with her husband and two children, one of whom is a teenager who has autism. Although her search for enlightenment often leads to bewilderment, she loves the adventure she receives as she is led on a romp back and forth between the world of autism and someplace a little more typical. She is currently the secretary of the Victoria Society for Children with Autism. She has a bachelor's degree in education, but has had a fondness for writing ever since she was a young girl who spent part of her summers in her parents' bookstore. This is the first novel she has completed. More could be on the way. "You never, never know."

ISBN 155212426-6
9 781552 124260